Sweet Dreams

Sweet Dreams

Sunny Leone

JUGGERNAUT BOOKS
KS House, 118 Shahpur Jat, New Delhi 110049, India

First published by Juggernaut Books 2016

Copyright © Sunny Leone 2016

All rights reserved. No part of this publication may be reproduced, transmitted, or stored in a retrieval system in any form or by any means without the written permission of the publisher.

ISBN 9788193237229

Typeset in Adobe Caslon Pro by R. Ajith Kumar, New Delhi

Printed at Manipal Technologies Ltd

Contents

7E	1
Dancer	17
New Year's Eve	33
Call Centre	51
The Cinema	67
The Neighbour	83
The One	97
The Massage	113
Rekindled Romance	125
The Gardener	139
Moon	159
Saying Goodbye	175
A Note on the Author	191

7E

There are moments in life that remain etched in your mind and which can never be erased. This story is about one I will be fantasizing about for years to come.

I work for a science centre based in New Delhi which consumes all my time and energy. The life of a researcher is mundane and unexciting to say the least. Dating and relationships have always taken a backseat to my career. But at that stage in my life, I was especially sure that men would never satisfy me the way work did. After all, I was a young, successful Indian woman who didn't rely on anyone else to get what I wanted – what could I possibly be missing?

I had just boarded a flight home after presenting a research paper on gene therapy at a conference in Bangalore. The presentation had gone off well but my energy was spent.

I knew it was just a matter of time before I was back in New Delhi in the comfort of my own home. The first thing I was going to do was take off the stiff, uncomfortable business suit I had been wearing all day and slip into one of my colourful and comfortable saris. The touch of the soft cotton on my skin always made me feel good. I wore my saris braless at home, which made me feel even more relaxed. At work, I would pair my demure office clothes with sexy undergarments made of lace and satin that always made my breasts feel perky and firm.

I couldn't get home fast enough.

The final passengers started boarding the plane. After a long and drawn-out day, I was hoping that the seat next to me would remain empty so I could enjoy a relaxing flight home. Little did I know that fate had other things in store for me that night.

I looked up and saw a tall, slender man standing in front of me, placing his luggage in the overhead haul. I could see his defined biceps tightening as he tried to shove his luggage into the bin. Something about his strength and determination made my heart race.

He sat down next to me and we made eye contact. It was only seconds but it felt so much longer.

He pulled out his laptop and started working instantly. His firm hands and fingers tapped the keyboard forcefully as he answered emails. It was like my heart was beating in sync with his typing. As he typed faster and harder my pulse kept pace and I found myself flustered and silently slipping into a heated trance.

What was it about this stranger that had me obsessing over him?

Without exchanging a word with him, I started weaving a story around the tall, dark and handsome man sitting next to me. He had to be a CEO or entrepreneur. Someone who had never been told no and had attained everything he'd ever wanted in life. Someone who enjoyed the best that life had to offer and had an insatiable thirst for its forbidden fruits.

His confident, piercing stare told me that he was someone who was always in charge when it came to work *or women*. He had delicate lips that had mastered the perfect degree of smirk and confidence, and his entire look signalled that he was someone who knew exactly what to say (or not to say) to get what he wanted. I could tell by looking at his soft hands and perfectly manicured nails that he knew just how important a gentle touch was in disarming the strength and will of someone he was pursuing. And all this with a hard body that he clearly spent endless hours honing into being a perfect specimen of the human form – it was just the tool he needed to dominate anyone who challenged him. He was a businessman who could close any deal, and a lover who could make any woman succumb to his desire.

Twenty minutes into the flight and I still couldn't stop thinking about the man who was sitting next to me. I thought a glass of hot tea and a good book would help me relax and maybe fall asleep. Instead it had the reverse effect and I started getting a little more courageous about expressing my admiration, sneaking long glances at him.

I knew that this was just a fun schoolgirl crush and when we landed I would never think about him again.

At one point, I noticed him rubbing the top of his leg as he steadily focused on reading what looked to be a business contract of some sort. It was probably just a nervous habit he had when he was focused on something, but I couldn't help but find it exhilarating. His lean, muscled hand rubbing himself, front to back to front to back, no doubt creating a warm friction on his thigh that was getting hotter with each firm stroke.

Then without warning he turned my way and caught me staring at his thighs.

He looked at me with a wicked smile and I began to blush. Trying to recover, I said that I had been admiring his watch and was looking for something similar as a gift for my father.

He started off on a story about a business trip to Germany where he had found the watch. I was so flustered I couldn't pay attention to the details of his story, but made appropriate facial expressions to let him know that I was interested.

A few minutes into his story he parted his legs slightly wider. I could feel the cool material of his pants now touching the bare skin of my knee.

He moved his hand on to his knee and then all of a sudden I could feel the warm sensation of his smooth, dark skin on mine. The tip of his ring finger was gently circling the top of my knee, sending a tingling sensation up my thigh.

I had to keep my composure so I made sure not to break eye contact with him and talked and acted like nothing was happening. But inside my heart was racing and my body was covered in goose bumps from his touch.

I was emotionally terrified. Here was a man who could clearly have any woman he wanted. His past love affairs most likely were with models and actresses or chic corporate women.

Why would he flirt with something like me? Was I reading more into this? Was he only accidentally touching me?

As my mind raced in confusion, he moved the subject to me and asked me in his beautiful, deep voice where I was travelling to.

Not being born with the gift of flirtation or small talk, I replied that I was flying home. I went into a nervous rant about the science research I was doing and I'm sure he didn't understand any of it. Embarrassed, I just stopped talking.

He leaned close to me and whispered that he was secretly a science nerd too, and not to tell anyone. I giggled like a schoolgirl and suddenly felt relaxed. The scent of his cologne lingered by my face for a few moments and I could feel the cabin getting warmer.

He began to talk about an article on global

warming he had read that morning in the *Times of India*, but all I could do was sit there and fantasize about his firm, lush lips hovering over my neck, which was sending me into a frenzy.

Then it hit me. I was his prey. He saw right through my naive distractions and his instincts told him that I wanted to be hunted. And he was right.

I nervously started to tell him another science story, but before I could even get a sentence out he had placed his finger on my lips and silently instructed me to stop talking. I couldn't resist opening my mouth slightly and nudging my tongue out just enough to taste the soft skin of his finger.

He slowly moved his fingers down my chin, past my throat, eventually arriving at my chest. I knew he could feel my heart pounding like a jackhammer at a construction site.

He leaned over and whispered for me to undo the top button of my blouse. I followed his instruction, and decided to go one step further and undo another button. But before I could he grabbed my hand and whispered to do exactly what he instructed me to do. Nothing *more*. Nothing *less*.

I looked around and everyone in the dimmed cabin

seemed to be asleep. No one was walking around and the stewardesses were chatting at the front of the cabin. I was safe but the feeling of being caught had only heightened the thrill.

My body temperature began to rise and a single drop of sweat started to form at the base of my neck and drip down slowly. Before it could come to the valley between my breasts, he gently wiped it off with his finger. Then he delicately sucked on the tip of his finger as if he had tasted the sweetness of honey.

He took my hand and I could feel my body melting as he tightly interlocked his fingers with mine. That simple gesture was like nothing I had ever felt before. My heart continued to beat faster as he stared deep into my eyes. Words couldn't describe the electric sensations that were pulsating through every nerve in my body.

I couldn't help but fantazise about what would happen next. I wanted nothing more than for him to use my body to fulfil all his animalistic desires. As the flight continued the passion between us grew more heated.

He instructed me to close my eyes and I willingly

complied. I could feel his warm breath on my neck. His lips were only inches away, filling me with anticipation. I could barely control myself as his lips finally made contact with my skin. My eyes were still closed but I could feel the sensation of his lips kissing my neck like the gentle flutter of butterfly wings.

I let out a quiet gasp as his wet tongue began to make its way up from the bottom of my neck to the top. My whole body was sweating with desire and I was paralysed with anticipation as I sat there awaiting his next instruction.

In a voice so quiet that it was almost inaudible he asked me to get up and make my way to the airplane lavatory.

I stood up and squeezed past him, my eyes never leaving his as I did so. Just as I was stepping on to the aisle I paused for a brief second, my breast looming dangerously close to his mouth. I could feel his warm breath penetrating the material of my blouse and I felt as if I was in a sauna.

Halfway down to the lavatory I could feel him staring at me, silently undressing me with his eyes as he followed behind. I entered and shut the door behind me and waited for what seemed an eternity for him to enter.

The door opened slowly and our eyes immediately locked. As he closed the door we had no other choice than to press our bodies firmly against each other. He turned around and grabbed the back of my head and swiftly brought our lips together.

His lips tasted like the sweet saltiness of a mango that I couldn't get enough of. As we kissed, our hands began to explore each other's bodies.

Impatiently he removed his belt and flung it forcefully to the floor. He pulled down his trousers, placed his hands on my waist and lifted me on to his body. My legs wrapped themselves around his waist like a tightly coiled snake, as our tongues tasted and wet each other's bodies.

As we stood there intertwined he ran his soft hands firmly down my back causing an electric sensation to shoot down my spine. His delicate touch discovering every part of my body opened me up to sensations I had never felt before.

I couldn't help but let out a gasp as I felt our bodies merging into one. Our hearts began to beat harder as our bodies moved together in a sensual rhythm.

As the rhythm between us gathered tempo, beads of sweat started to form all over our bodies, forcing us to hold on to each other harder as our glistening bodies grew slippery.

Our eyes made contact as if our souls were meant to be one. The pleasure our bodies had been longing for from the moment we first met had finally been fulfilled. We stood there gasping for air as we remained intertwined with one another.

Without saying a word, we started to pull ourselves apart. Before exiting he pulled me towards him. My body was still trembling from the passionate encounter. He leaned down and gently pressed his lips against mine. I knew it was the last time I would ever get to enjoy the sweetness of his luscious lips. It was an experience so unreal that I knew my body would never feel that satisfaction again.

As he left I took a moment to look at myself in the mirror. My hair was dishevelled, the top button of my blouse ripped and my skirt crumbled. I straightened myself up as much as I could and wondered if people would sense what had just happened. Luckily I had a jacket to cover up my indiscretions.

On the way back to my seat I heard the pilot

announcing that we were about to approach our destination. I squeezed back into my seat, my back towards him. We didn't make eye contact or speak a word for the rest of the flight. In the dark, silent cabin, I closed my eyes and replayed the lovemaking that had just occurred. It was a scene so unreal that I had to remind myself that this wasn't just some fantasy. My beating heart, my sweat-stained body were evidence.

We landed and just as we were about to get up from our seats he leaned over, one more time, to whisper goodbye in my ear. I could feel his breath teasing my body one last time.

I turned to him so our eyes could meet. I hungrily tried to capture every detail of his face so it would remain deep in my memory. He stood up, grabbed his bag from the bin and started walking to the exit. My eyes followed him and, just before he walked out of the plane, he turned and looked at me one last time.

Then he was gone. I knew we would go back to our normal lives, never to see one another again.

That incident would be something that would get me through the loneliest times in my life. Maybe I was just one of many girls in his sexual conquests, maybe he has forgotten my face. But I will never forget him. His beautiful dark skin, his forceful but delicate touch, and the sweet taste of his wet kisses will be with me forever.

Dancer

I am a software engineer working in New York. They say it's the city that never sleeps but I have never really had the chance to play here. Instead I spent my years putting every ounce of energy into my work.

I stayed late, worked weekends, even through most holidays. My supervisors praised my dedication, which was so peculiar to me. Constantly working was the only thing I grew up knowing in my low-income family where both my parents worked, struggling to educate us kids. Getting ahead was the mantra I had grown up by.

As the years went by this mantra helped me score in exams, win scholarships and climb the corporate ladder. Within six years of being employed I was promoted to VP, running the entire software development division of the company and in charge of about a hundred-odd engineers.

It was wonderful to now be able to take care of my parents. My father could work fewer hours in his shop, and my mother was able to quit her job and just focus on running the home. I spoke to them on the phone once every week or two when I had some free time.

My mother was persistent about me going home to visit. I wanted to see my family, but something or the other always came up and I could never make it. Besides there were some subjects I wanted to avoid – such as women.

Relationships were always a topic I dreaded to talk about during our calls. Now in my thirties, the pressure was on to get married, buy a house and have children. But it wasn't that simple. I didn't have the time to meet a woman. It was almost like I was in a relationship with my job. I tried to convey this to my family as best I could, but I don't think they understood. They just didn't want me to be lonely.

In reality I was far from lonely. While work consumed a lot of time, there are ways that single men in my status fill the void of not having a girlfriend or wife. Every weekend me and a group of executives from our office made our way down to a bar called The Spot.

The Spot only allowed men to enter. It was very exclusive, and catered to the wealthy elite of New York. A typical bar tab would run to $1200 a night and that didn't include money spent on entertainment. Their selection of wine and liquor was exquisite. But people didn't go there for the drinks.

When you walked in all you could see was a sea of business suits surrounding a neon-lit stage. This was the main stage where each night men would gather around for a special performance. Men sitting around with wads of hundred dollar bills in their hands anxiously awaiting an exotic beauty to appear on the stage.

The ladies were always stunning. Slim frames, curvaceous hips, and large, round breasts that bounced around as they did their little performances. The Spot's performers were mostly women of white ethnicity. On a few occasions I recall seeing a few Asian and black girls. But for the most part the men had an appetite for the busty, blonde bombshells.

In the beginning these beauties were completely foreign to me. Back in India, the only places I saw ladies like that were in adult movies or magazines. But even they were nothing in comparison to these girls.

I learned here that everything could be bought for the right price. Even the overweight and ugly businessmen could leave with the most attractive woman in the room.

Aside from the main performer, The Spot had another twenty ladies that walked around making sure the businessmen were enjoying themselves. They would bring them drinks, sit on their laps and for the right amount go home with them at the end of the night.

These girls were the perfect solution to the built-up sexual frustration that workaholics like myself needed to release. One or two nights a week I would pay one of the sexy ladies to come back to my place for a late night drink. To have the featured performer go home with you would cost you anywhere from $10,000 to $25,000 for the night depending on who was bidding. This was well out of my range but I found enough pleasure in taking home one of the side ladies. Usually $3000 plus drinks and dinner secured me some action for the night.

It was a perfect arrangement. I took them back to

my place, fooled around for a few hours, then arranged a private car to take her home. Feeling satiated, I would shower, check my email then head off to bed.

This happened so frequently that I started losing the perception of how normal relationships worked. Flirting wasn't necessary. Trying to win a girl's attention or figure out if she liked me didn't seem to matter any more. I had the money, I got what I wanted, and we were done. It was on to the next pretty toy to stimulate my body's desires.

One evening I hit up The Spot with my colleagues. It seemed to be just another ordinary night with the guys. We headed in and went straight for the bar. To get us started we did three rapid-fire shots of tequila, one after another.

A booth had opened up near the main stage so we quickly made our way through the crowd to get ready for the show. The host announced that there would be a new performer that night called Vivica.

Surely Vivica was just a clone of the blonde bombshells that we saw each week, but it was still exciting to hear there was some new flesh in the bar. The name too sounded close to home.

As the lights dimmed, an orange spotlight hit

the stage. Music started to play. But it wasn't the jazz style music that usually played during these performances. It was something familiar, one which instantly stimulated my body. It was a Bollywood song, a cool remix of an old hit that I had loved as a kid. Immediately my interest was sparked.

The sounds were new and tantalizing to the men, and they gave a loud roar as anticipation built. Who was going to come out to dance to this strange, exotic music?

As a hand began to pull back the curtain, the crowd of men became completely silent. All eyes were glued to the stage. Then suddenly this exotic, dark-skinned beauty with long, silky hair and large, brown eyes stood before us. Her body was decorated with little crystals, and she was wearing a sheer sari that barely covered her private parts.

I'd never seen a sari draped like this back home. There was barely any material to go around Vivica's body, and her right breast was partially exposed, giving us a tantalizing glimpse of its delicious roundness. The outfit had a slit that ran all the way up to her waist, with nothing but a thin layer of sheer covering her firm leg. Her hands, neck and ears were covered in sparkling diamonds and gold – this was a treasure like none of us had seen before.

Vivica danced sinfully around the stage, her sari struggling to conceal the intimate parts of her body, her hips moving seductively to the beat. The men were mesmerized by her exotic sex appeal and the way she moved her body. The room was enamoured, waiting in bated breath for her next move. I had never seen so much sexual tension in The Spot before. Vivica had every man in her palms.

Her performance ended and the room erupted into loud cheers. The gorgeous dancer, standing statuesque on the stage, stood there taking it all in with a knowing smile. She knew exactly the effect she had on us all.

The men, all turned on, started pulling out their wallets. It was time to bid on who would be taking this exotic beauty home. This was usually my time to step aside but I knew I had to take her home that night. There was no way a treasure like this should be going home with some raunchy, fat businessman.

No one in the room could appreciate the true beauty of an Indian woman like I could. The appeal of an Indian woman is not just in her bare skin, it's her spiritual aura, her loyalty to her family, her warmth. This girl may have looked like a goddess, she may barely have had any clothes on, but I could immediately sense there was something more special about her.

The bidding war started. Within minutes the room was up to $25,000; it was like nothing I had seen before. As soon as I made a bid, someone bid $10,000 higher.

Quickly I realized I was playing with the big boys in the room. Bidding slowed down as we reached $40,000. The smell of that much money caused the side girls to start circling the high bidders in an effort to get the money for them. They were like vultures circling an animal in its last moments.

Knowing I was out of my league I made one last bid at $45,000. It was a last shot, but it was all the money I had to spend and I hoped that it was enough. Seconds passed by. The host made one final call for another bidder. Trying to play it cool, I took a sip from my drink and casually looked around the room. Then I heard the word 'SOLD'.

I couldn't believe it: the exotic beauty that every man in the room wanted was going home with me. I paid the host and was escorted to a private table where Vivica was waiting.

We exchanged introductions. She seemed a bit cold, as if she was numb to the whole process. I tried to initiate conversation with her but she would just answer quickly, smile, then look away.

The Spot was closing up. I took her hand and we made our way outside and waited for the car to pick us up. The entire ride was silent. This wasn't the typical experience I was used to, and didn't really understand why she was so stand-offish.

We arrived at my place. I paid the driver, then headed up the elevator. I unlocked the door and gestured for her to go inside. I immediately headed to the bar to fix us some drinks, while she made her way to the couch. I tried to make her comfortable, to engage her in small talk, but nothing really worked.

We sat there in silence for some time with our drinks. I was on the verge of giving up on my evening when she looked up at me and started to talk. She said she was sorry that I had to spend so much money on her, that $45,000 seemed like a ridiculous amount of money to spend on a night with one person.

I leaned forward and looked directly into her eyes

and told her the truth, that I couldn't bear for anyone else to spend even a minute with her. For the first time, she smiled and her eyes opened wide, and she looked even more beautiful than before.

She told me I was different from the other men that she had been with. There was something kind about me. Her comment took me back. What kind of life had she lived, I wondered, if someone like me seemed foreign to her?

I pictured the type of guys from The Spot and their stories about the degrading things they made the girls do. That wasn't something I was ever into, even their stories made me feel uneasy.

This was the world Vivica knew. I felt bad for her. I had spent a ridiculous amount of money to bring her home, but now it felt wrong. She wasn't like the other girls who just wanted some quick cash and gave no emotion to the time we spent together. I leaned forward and grabbed her hands. I told her she didn't have to sleep with me.

A concerned look came over her face and she started to tell me The Spot would find out and take action against her. I assured her they would never know and asked her to make me a promise, to take the money she made that night and try to find another line of work.

Her eyes started tearing up. Then she mumbled the name 'Anaya'. Before I could ask who Anaya was, she told me it was her real name. She had spent the first half of her life living in Mumbai before her father got a job in the US.

The tension that had been between us all night was gone. As we talked more, about our lives back in India, a familiar feeling came over us. We had a few drinks and even danced a little. I pulled out a few CDs of popular song items from my favourite Bollywood flicks and Anaya's face lit up. There was no one in New York that I was able to relate to on that level, no one who appreciated Indian culture. It felt nice to have someone who shared some of those interests.

As the night grew, the chemistry between us started to change. By connecting on a personal level an attraction had started to form. At one point I sat down with a glass of wine and watched her dancing in front of the window, her diamond and gold jewellery sparkling like little stars as she floated around the room.

She moved with such grace and confidence, as if

she were a goddess enchanting me with her dancing. Her hips swaying in a circular motion started to get me aroused. As my body heated up, it felt as if the room was on fire. I undid the top buttons of my shirt, trying to stay calm.

Anaya knew exactly what she was doing to me. With her sari flowing behind her, she slowly walked towards my direction. Kneeling down in front of me, she grabbed my thighs firmly with her hands. She leaned forward and planted a delicate kiss on my lips. With our bodies inches away from one another, she whispered in my ear that she wanted to make love.

I stood up, gently placing my hands around her waist as I pulled her up towards me. I began kissing her neck. The scent of her perfume was so intoxicating, something I couldn't get enough of. She began to moan lightly as my lips made their way down her neck. She removed her pallu, exposing her soft, ample breasts and placed my hands on them. I delicately squeezed her breasts, sending shudders through her body.

I started removing my clothes. As I stood there naked in front of Anaya, I could see an overwhelming sense of passion glaze over her face. At that moment she wanted nothing more than my body to fulfil her every desire.

We started to kiss passionately. I made Anaya lean against the wall, our bodies pressed tightly together as I entered her. She couldn't help but let out loud moans of pleasure with each passionate thrust.

Tasting the saltiness of her skin, our bodies began to move in a rhythm as if we were one. At times she took control, moving her body in a circular motion. My body began to shake with pleasure. I asked her to slow down, but she knew that she had me to the point of ecstasy. Her dance had me in a total frenzy.

Our bodies, exhausted from a night of passion, drenched in perspiration, approached our sexual peak. As we finished, we passionately kissed one another. Her legs were wrapped firmly around my waist, my hands tangled in her beautiful, dark locks of hair. We stood there for a few minutes longer, lost in the labyrinth of our passion, our bodies still as one.

That was the first of many nights that I would spend with Anaya. There was an amazing chemistry between the two of us, something that couldn't be bought with money. As the months went by the dynamics of our encounters changed. I stopped going to The Spot and she stopped performing there. While we enjoyed our late night sinful adventures, we started spending time together at the park and going to dinner. I began to learn to truly play in this great big sleeping city. The sexual chemistry that brought us together too began to change into something much deeper.

Almost a year after we met, we decided to make a life-changing commitment. We made plans to move back to Mumbai so we could spend more time with each other and our families. Money just didn't seem to be important any more. I'm still amazed how fate brought the complicated worlds of two lonely souls together to share a lifetime of love.

New Year's Eve

All my life I never felt beautiful. I was overweight, frumpy and the farthest thing away from looking like the beauties plastered on every magazine cover or movie poster.

I was sick and tired of being labelled the 'nice girl'. Not that I disliked being a nice person. I just longed for other characteristics that mattered most to men.

My family was particularly disparaging with their relentless use of cruel nicknames for me like 'chubby', 'cow' and 'moti'. I was constantly compared to my cousins who were of a similar age. They had smooth, soft, brown skin, long legs and beautiful hair that was always perfectly styled. I could never compete with them, nor did I want to.

For the last nineteen years I had waited for fate to bring me the beauty I had longed for all my life.

Beauty that would give me the confidence men were attracted to.

One New Year's Eve my life changed. Something happened that forced me to take fate into my own hands and be the person I always wanted to be.

The party was in full swing, and I was having a wonderful time at my friend Priya's house in Bandra. Music was blasting through the apartment, the smell of delicious food wafted through the air, and the place was full of stylish young men and women.

For once, I was feeling particularly attractive. That morning I had spent hours at the salon getting my make-up done. My hair was the picture of perfection – pulled back into a sleek, smooth ponytail and decorated with a gold headpiece I had borrowed from a cousin. I wore the most beautiful sari, full of shimmering sequin detailing that made me sparkle like a star. The sari was a fiery red, but the colour would occasionally flash like a hot sunset through the sequins. There was never a moment in my life when I had felt more exquisite.

As midnight approached, my eyes were drawn to a man across the room. He had short, sexy hair, which was perfectly styled. His clothes, tailored to

New Year's Eve

his fit body so that it showed off every muscle, and his chiselled face were the combination of someone straight out of a Bollywood film.

For the next thirty minutes I silently stalked him with my eyes. As he moved around the room, my eyes remained glued to him, unable to tear away from that handsome man. My friend was talking to me and I pretended to listen, but really all I could focus on was the deep, rugged sound of his voice booming across the room. I could hear it getting louder as he made his way to the drinks table where I was standing.

He was now standing just inches away from me. My body started to tense up and my heart began to beat faster. No one had ever made me feel this way before.

As much as I longed to exchange words with him, I knew I was invisible to him. There were far more beautiful girls at the party just waiting for the chance to hang on to his arm.

Then it happened – we made eye contact. I'm sure I was blushing like a little girl talking to her first crush. There was nothing I could do. I was too enamoured so I just stood there staring. Like a gentleman, he smiled and gave me a wink. It was an unexpected gesture that only made him more attractive in my eyes.

In a soft, deep voice, he introduced himself as Asif and asked if I was enjoying myself at the party. I told him my name was Alia and that I was having a great time, especially since he was there. It took every ounce of courage to speak so boldly. Had I made a complete fool of myself?

Paralysed with the fear of rejection, I waited for his response. It was only a second but it felt like an eternity. Then he let out a small laugh and thanked me, and said that he too felt the same way.

I knew he was lying. But his kindness in not wanting to hurt my feelings just made my attraction to him grow further. He said he had to get back to his friends but would catch up with me before the night ended. I told him I would like that, and he made his way back through the crowd.

I couldn't believe it. My luck had finally changed. No longer would I be the sad girl who was destined to be a lonely spinster, like my family always suggested. At nineteen, I had become a woman who was in charge of her own destiny, *or so I thought*.

The New Year was almost upon us and I was

making my way back from the restroom. I heard Asif's voice just as I was about to come around the corner. I stopped so I could listen to his voice one more time and learn something about him.

He and his friends were talking about who was going to be their New Year's kiss. I heard one of his friends ask him about the girl he was talking to earlier when he was getting a drink.

They were talking about me??? My smile probably stretched from ear to ear. Could it be that I was going to experience my first kiss? And that it would be on New Year's with the most handsome man?

My fingers coiled so tightly that my hands began to perspire as I waited for his response. He replied, 'No, she's too fat.' I heard the outburst of laughter as my eyes filled up with tears. He had destroyed everything in one quick second.

I rushed back to the restroom, weeping uncontrollably. As I stood there completely crushed, I could hear the loud, joyous voices at the party starting the countdown as the clock ticked towards midnight.

'5 — 4 — 3 — 2 — 1 — Happy New Year!'

I could well imagine the scene outside, with friends hugging and kissing, and discussing their hopes and resolutions for the year that had just arrived. I stood in the restroom feeling more pathetic as each miserable minute passed by.

Somehow I managed to pull myself together and fight back the tears. I washed off the sad trails of mascara that had run down my cheeks and desperately tried to refresh my face. I prayed that no one could see that I was a shattered mess inside.

Leaving the restroom, I made my way through the party. I could hear my friends calling my name but I remained focused on the door. I had to get out as soon as possible before the tears started up again.

Only a few feet from the door I could sense Asif standing just to my right. My instincts told me to keep looking forward and walk right past him. But of course I couldn't. I had to take just one more look at the stranger who had broken my heart into a million pieces. My eyes instantly started to tear up as my head turned towards him.

At that very moment he turned my way and our eyes made contact. He could see that something was wrong by my eyes shining now with tears. As our eyes connected it was clear he knew why I was upset.

New Year's Eve

But, without an ounce of compassion, he turned away from me and returned to his conversation. This act was just as hurtful, if not more, as the cruel comments he had made earlier.

The next couple of months were some of the worst of my life. I locked myself in my room, stopped answering calls from friends and made no effort to make myself presentable.

My mind kept replaying what had happened that torturous New Year's. Pain couldn't penetrate my heart any more because there was nothing left except a void of emptiness.

Then one day something odd happened. The heaviness that had blanketed my body lifted. The sadness that had taken up home in my eyes vanished. My heart started to beat again and I could feel life course through my veins.

My mind still replayed the events of that horrible night. But instead of remembering my bitter pain, I started to remember the way I had felt at the beginning of the night. The fun conversations I had with my friends, how beautiful my hair and make-up looked and how stunning my sari was. In that moment

I realized that it wasn't too late for my life to change. To appreciate the good things in life I would have to endure the pain as well.

I spent the next six months channelling all my energy into the gym and putting myself through a tough diet plan. I knew that getting my body in shape was critical to feeling better about myself.

Each week I could feel my body changing. My waist was starting to narrow and my stomach started to get firmer and firmer. My cheekbones and jawline started to get more defined, and my skin looked smoother and began to glow. I began to like the way I looked in the mirror.

I went out and got myself a completely new wardrobe. I only bought clothing that accentuated my body and I wasn't scared to wear pieces that were more revealing. Picking out beautiful bras and panties became an obsession of mine. I loved lingerie made of lace and soft silk that felt cool against my skin and drew attention to my breasts, which had always been my favourite feature.

I started to work on my social life again. Friends I hadn't seen in a while were shocked when they saw the

New Year's Eve

transformation and applauded my hard work. I began dating guys around my neighbourhood, but not too seriously. I wasn't ready to let anyone get close enough to me where they could break my heart.

A friend of mine decided to play matchmaker and was confident that he had found the perfect man for me. A successful engineer with a good family and extremely attractive – what wasn't to like?

I agreed and he set up the date for the upcoming Saturday at a hip restaurant down the street from where I lived. I spent the next few days shopping for the perfect outfit. I have always loved saris and found one in a lovely pink with gold accents and paired it with a sexy, wide-necked blouse that showed off my stomach and shoulders. It was old-fashioned of me to wear a sari to a date but I knew it accentuated my curves, and made me look my voluptuous best.

Saturday evening arrived. As I put the finishing touches to my make-up, I sat back and let myself just be in the moment. I walked down the stairs and my mother gasped and placed her hands over her mouth. She just looked at me and smiled tearfully and told me that she had never seen a more beautiful creature.

My mother had NEVER told me I was beautiful. I was so in shock I didn't know how to respond except by giving her a hug.

The doorbell rang. I grabbed my shawl and purse and proceeded to greet my date who was being ushered in by the maid. Standing in front of me was Asif from the party. It was like seeing a ghost from the past. I stood there expressionless and could feel the blood draining from my face.

He said his name was Asif and he was there to meet Alia. I quickly slapped a smile on my face and introduced myself. Almost a year had passed since the party and it was clear he didn't remember me.

On the way to the restaurant, he attempted to make small talk, but my brain couldn't register anything he was saying. He had no idea who I was. No idea that he was the reason I had slipped into a depression for months.

I decided that I wasn't going to give him the power to make me feel insecure like he had done before, and I certainly wasn't going to run away crying like I had. I would not even let him ruin this night for me.

We ordered our food and drinks and once I had gulped down my first glass of chilled white wine

New Year's Eve

I started to get more comfortable. The nice guy I remembered had taken over and swept his way a little back into my heart. We spent most of the evening laughing and being silly. And as the evening went by, all my old feelings reappeared. His smell, his voice, his eyes played havoc with my heart and body. Even as I made conversation, I could feel myself becoming excited.

We left the restaurant and took a long walk by the sea, on Marine Drive. Neither of us wanted that night to end. We found a bench and sat for a while, watching the other couples flirt, the kids play with their parents as the sea breeze caressed our faces. He grabbed my hand and our fingers interlocked. He leaned over and gave me a sweet kiss on my lips. His lips were softer than anything I had ever felt before.

My eyes were calling out for him to kiss me again and so he did. We kissed passionately on that bench as people walked by. His kiss was exactly as I had imagined it would be. Then in a deep voice so familiar to my ears he asked me to come back to his apartment which was down the road.

My lips trembled as I tried to say no. This was my moment to tell him why, but my heart had made up its own mind and I heard myself say a breathless yes.

With his soft, gentle hand, he took mine and led me to his place. With each step my heart began to beat faster and faster. The night air was warm, but couldn't compare to the heat I was feeling in my body, the tightness in my stomach.

He unlocked his door with a determined ease. As soon as we both were inside he shut the door and placed his hands around my face. He brought his lips to mine and we kissed passionately like long-lost lovers that had just been reunited.

Our lips took a break just long enough for him to turn his head towards his bedroom. He looked back at me to see if I wanted the same thing. My legs began to go weak from anticipation and excitement as he slowly guided me to his bedroom.

He stared deep into my eyes as he started to unbutton his shirt. I placed my hands on his chest, slowing working them to his shoulders before flinging his shirt to the floor.

The next few minutes he spent slowly removing my sari, unwinding each layer. His fingers gently caressed my skin as he undressed me. Each touch was so delicate as if he thought my body was made of thin glass that would shatter if he was too rough. He unbuckled his belt and removed his pants.

Now undressed, I stood shyly in my lace bra and panties. I had chosen one of my favourite pairs – made of red lace, as red as the sari I had worn to that New Year's Eve. I felt his eyes devour every part of my body. I felt vulnerable, and suddenly unattractive.

I couldn't help but take in the perfection of his body. His thick, muscular legs stood firm and his strong arms were waiting to grab my waist. I felt small next to him and weak with desire.

He put his hand behind my neck and slowly laid me down on his bed. I leaned over to his nightstand to turn off the light, but before I could he stopped me.

I whispered to him that I was not comfortable with my body. In a deep whisper back he told me that my body was perfection and he couldn't bear to take his eyes off me for a single second.

We began to kiss passionately. Our lips never left the surface of one another's skin as we explored the most sensual parts of our bodies. Our bodies collided with the passion. Every movement of our bodies was in sync with one another. His breath grew deeper as he used every muscle in his body to bring me to ecstasy.

I began to moan – the non-stop rhythms of our

lovemaking set my body aflame. My hands holding on to his back were like the claws of a panther clinging to its prey. As he filled my body with pleasure, my fingers dug deeper into his glowing, dark skin.

The room was filled with the scent of lust as we inched closer and closer to fulfilling our animalistic desires. As he brought us to ecstasy, the bed started to rattle, our hearts began racing, and we both began to moan loudly.

I had never felt such sensation before. It was like electricity running through my veins. We lay there for what seemed like forever, kissing each other. I could've stayed like that for days. His body on top of mine, my legs still firmly wrapped around his waist. My heart melted as he kissed my neck and shoulders so passionately before falling asleep in exhaustion.

I couldn't explain why, but as my heart began to calm and the tingling sensation stopped coursing through my body, I felt a heaviness in my soul. Seeing his sleeping face, I was reminded of his cruelty, which seemed at such odds with his beauty. The pain I felt on New Year's started to rush back through my body. Our night had become just a memory and I realized that nothing more would ever come from our encounter.

New Year's Eve

My heart wouldn't let go of that New Year's night.

I got out of bed and headed quietly to the restroom to make myself presentable. I grabbed my shawl and purse and headed to the door. Just as my hand touched the doorknob he called my name and I froze. I had hoped to make a swift exit but it was not to be.

As if he knew he would never see me again, he grabbed my hand and said goodbye. I smiled at him but said nothing. Before I could make my way through the door he called my name one more time.

He told me that when he saw me as he walked in through the door for our date, all he could think of was how beautiful I was. He said it was also what he thought when he first met me at the New Year party. In his deep voice he murmured that he was sorry about that evening as I turned and made my way home. I was in such shock I couldn't respond.

As my taxi sped down Marine Drive taking me home, I lowered my window and let the wind tousle my hair. The radio was playing a sad, sweet love song and I asked the grumpy old taxi driver to increase the volume. The road was empty, the sea alive, the song reverberating in the car. I felt happy and sad, alone and complete. I would never forget the magical night we had spent together but I would never go back. I knew then what role this beautiful man had played in my life – he was the reason I became a woman.

Call Centre

My name is Dilpreet. I have the fascinating job of being a call centre representative at a fancy software company in Bangalore. Really, quite the opposite. I spend eight hours a day sitting at a cubicle taking call after call from people asking the same questions.

Don't get me wrong – I like my job. I have a steady income with okay perks. The customers are mostly pleasant and I am fascinated by their American accents. They usually laugh when they hear my name. See, in our call centre we are required to have a name similar to our predominantly American customers. My name is 'Peter'. They think people will feel more comfortable talking to a Peter than to a Dilpreet, even though most of the clients I speak to don't believe for a second that it is my real name.

When I joined, the entire call centre was overseen

by the Senior Call Centre Executive. Her name was Kalpana. She was stunning. She had the type of beauty that men couldn't help stare at the minute she entered a room. We all knew she also was on a fast track to bigger and better things – and that the CEO saw her as his protégée. So she was smart, successful and hot as hell. What a combination. Everyone was intimidated by Kalpana's subtle yet sexy confidence. The men fantasized what it would be like to be with her, and the ladies fantasized what it would be like to be her.

No man in our call centre had even a remote chance to be with her. She was a perfect 10 with a high-paying career and a brand-new shiny black Audi. The city's most elite bachelors were at her beck and call.

Six months into my job at the call centre, something happened that completely turned my world around.

I got to work and there seemed to be a cloud of tension hanging over the centre. Some colleagues were huddled around the water cooler so I walked over and asked if they knew what was going on. They mentioned that one of the shift supervisors had quit and taken four members from her team with her.

The call centre was staffed to cover just what was needed to make sure all the calls were answered in a timely manner. The loss of four employees and a supervisor would have a huge impact on the company. Call quotas would not be met, which meant no bonuses. Even people who wanted to take just a day off would be affected.

As I sat answering phones at my cubicle I could hear Kalpana's high-heeled shoes clicking up and down the aisles. Maybe she was looking for someone to cover the shift of those who had left. I wasn't sure but grew more curious as I heard those shoes working their way closer and closer to my cubicle.

Then it happened. As I was talking to 'John from Dallas, Texas' about why his debit card had got blocked I could smell the scent of jasmine surrounding me. My heart started to beat faster. My hands started to sweat as I saw Kalpana's hourglass figure behind me reflected on my monitor.

She had never come into my cubicle before. In fact, she had never even been that close to me before. I knew it was my one chance to make a memorable first impression.

As I turned around and promptly jumped up to greet her, the unthinkable happened. I hadn't removed my headphones. And before I knew it, I was yanked back by the cord from the headset and was on the floor.

There I was, laid out like a human rug, making a fool of myself in front of the hottest woman in the office. Kalpana was looking down at me with her hands covering her mouth, desperately trying to hold back her laughter. Others who had heard the loud crash were now peeking in and over my cubicle to see what had happened. It was a nightmare except it was real. I would be teased for a month at least.

I lifted my head up and asked Kalpana if there was something I could help her with. Still trying to control her giggles, she composed herself long enough to ask if I was interested in helping her train some new employees the following week. Still lying on the floor, I smiled and said yes.

She thanked me and asked me to go to her office when my shift was over. As she made her way back to her office, I could feel the vibrations of her heels on the floor. And it set my heart racing.

All I could think was how lucky I was that the office beauty had asked me to help her out! Maybe it was a chance for me to get promoted. Maybe it was a stepping-stone to a high-level position where she would actually consider going on a date with me. Not likely, but it's always fun to fantasize.

I began my countdown to the end of my shift. The last fifteen minutes were moving so slow. It was as if time had stood still as I waited anxiously for each minute to change to the next.

Finally, I was off. I was going to be face-to-face with Kalpana in just a few minutes. My nerves started to kick in as I wondered if I looked presentable, if my breath was okay and if I had remembered to put deodorant on in the morning.

I grabbed my stuff and ran to the restroom. Looking in the mirror, I wet my hands and tried to work my hair into a trendy style but it didn't work. Using only a finger and the faucet I tried to give my teeth a quick brush. I couldn't get the smell off from the day's lunch. I unwrapped four pieces of gum and tossed them into my mouth and started chewing.

Time was just speeding by. I looked at my watch and realized I had spent ten minutes getting ready in the restroom. The funny thing was I looked exactly the same as I had when I went in, but now had minty breath.

Before making my way to Kalpana's office I

practised greeting her about fifteen times in the mirror. Finally, I mustered up the courage and bolted out of the door. I walked into her office, sat down and said nothing. What was wrong with me? Why couldn't my brain send the message to my mouth to say something!

As we sat there staring at each other, her face broke into a gorgeous smile. She thanked me for helping her and emphasized how important this was for the company.

We sat there for a few hours going over a strategy on training new employees and getting them up to speed as soon as possible. I somehow managed to move past my infatuation with Kalpana and focus on the training plan. By the time we were done, the entire floor had emptied out. The two of us sat in a sea of darkness with empty offices and cubicles surrounding us.

I could tell Kalpana was getting more comfortable with me. She had gathered her hair into a messy bun. Kicked off her shoes and had her feet up on a chair. This was surprising because she always seemed so formal and was always perfectly put-together. But I liked it.

As we took a break from work and walked to the

soft drinks machine to grab some Coke, we got talking about music and movies. Like me, she was a fan of old Bollywood movies and we compared our favourite actors and songs.

Kalpana was at least fifteen years older than me, but it didn't feel like that as we began to slowly tease each other and make wisecracks. As strange as it may sound, our training session started to feel like a date. And not just any date, a good one.

It was close to midnight when she asked if I needed to go home. I had had a long day at work but being with her had given me a burst of energy. Trying to play it cool, I casually told her I didn't mind taking one for the team.

She laughed. Something about the way she laughed was so sexy. I found myself trying hard to say stupid little things just so I could hear her laugh. She said she'd never met someone like me and she wasn't sure if that was a good thing, looking coyly at the floor as she said so.

She was flirting with me! I couldn't believe it! She looked up at me and asked if I could keep a secret. I responded with a confident yes and asked her what it was.

Was it some good office gossip that only the top-level people knew about? Was I going to be promoted as the new supervisor?

She looked at me for a few minutes, not saying a word. Then, slowly reaching into the cabinet next to her desk, she pulled out a bottle of wine. She smiled naughtily and shrugged her shoulders as if she was a teenager who had just sneaked out a bottle of liquor from her parents' stash.

Alcohol was not allowed in the workplace under any circumstances. Well, maybe those were the rules only for the lesser paid employees. She asked if I minded her having a few sips. I said not at all, I completely understood, it had been a long, stressful day and she should do whatever it took to relax…

She resourcefully used a mail opener to open the bottle. I was very impressed.

There weren't any glasses around so she just took a few swigs from the bottle. Without saying a word, she pointed the bottle towards me. Trying to be a mature, cool adult I grabbed the bottle and took a big gulp.

I didn't really have a taste for wine, being mostly a beer and whisky guy. Still I suffered through it, going back and forth with Kalpana taking drink after drink.

After a while, the taste wasn't that bad. We finished the whole bottle before deciding to get back to work. It was fun but it was critical we got back on track for the upcoming training.

Kalpana got up and brought over an agenda for the training schedule. Standing right next to me, she placed the schedule on the table in front of me. She leaned over and started going over ideas on how to rate the trainees on test calls as part of the training. Honestly, I had no idea what she was talking about. All I could think about was her arm against mine as she talked. I felt her body heat, her hair that had fallen over her face, and my blood started pulsating through my veins.

I discreetly stole a look and got a glimpse of her ample breasts straining against her white cotton blouse. Standing beside her, our heads bent over the table, I prayed she couldn't tell I was aroused. Maybe it was the effect of the wine, the late night, but I couldn't help being turned on by her every move.

Still talking about the training in a soft voice, she turned around and sat on the desk right next to me. Now she was facing me and I had to do everything in my power to stay focused on her eyes and words.

She had crossed her legs. Her tight-fitting grey skirt had moved quite high above her knees. It had got cold in the office and she started to rub her legs against each other in a slow, sensual manner to warm herself.

As she stopped to check some emails on her phone, I couldn't resist taking a quick look at her long, sexy legs. I slowly inched back in my seat until I caught a glimpse of her panties. My heart began to pound and my breathing got a little heavier.

Noticing my shallow breathing, she asked if I was okay. I quickly shrugged it off saying that I was feeling a little faint from the wine. Kalpana insisted on dragging me over to the little couch on the other side of her office to rest. She laid me down and placed her hand on my forehead. The touch of her soft hands on my skin suffused my entire body with a warm sensation.

She said I felt warm and should take a minute to relax. Her hands moved from my forehead to my cheeks, then on to my neck. Undoing two of my shirt buttons, she began to run her palms in a gentle circular motion on my chest.

I lay there on the couch with Kalpana leaning over

me. I was excited but completely terrified. My body was paralysed with fear and desire.

There was no hiding that I was fully aroused. Would she get upset? Would I get fired? She made her way down my chest and past my stomach, gently grazing my manhood as her fingers lingered on my thighs. I realized she was taunting me with her touch. This wasn't an innocent display of concern – she was making a pass at me.

She stood over me and began to unbutton her blouse, slowly removing it and letting it drop on to the floor. Her breasts spilled over her bra and I could only think of ripping it away with my mouth. Her hands made their way to her waist and she began to slowly unzip her skirt. Kalpana kneeled down and placed her lips on mine. We began to kiss passionately. I was so hungry now that I felt like an animal.

I could feel her firm body on mine. My fingers began to work their way from the top of her back down to her buttocks. Her smooth, dark skin felt like silk on my fingertips. She sat up and undid her bra, revealing her beautiful ample breasts.

She noticed the slightly tense look on my face and asked if I wanted her to stop. I paused before giving her an answer. It wasn't that I wanted to stop. I had never been with a woman before, intimately, and I was embarrassed. Would I be able to satisfy this beautiful older woman?

When I found the courage to tell her, she just looked at me with that sexy smile of hers and said not to worry. She would teach me how to be a lover.

She unbuckled my belt, and slowly began to remove my pants. Her hands made sure not to leave any part of my body untouched. I placed my hands on her bare breasts. They were softer than I could have imagined. The sensation of my gentle fingers navigating around her breast made her shiver and moan, and I could see goose bumps had appeared all over her body.

As she sat on top of me I could feel her body start to move in a circular rhythm, working my body into an uncontrollable frenzy. She let out a faint moan as I entered her. The rhythm of our bodies picked up pace.

Suddenly intimacy wasn't so new to me. It felt like the most natural thing in the world. I stood up with Kalpana still on top of me, her legs wrapped around me. I carried her to the desk and gently laid her down.

She looked up at me, her eyes dark with desire, as I began to lead this dance of passion. The desk shook unsteadily as my body moved back and forth in quick swaying motions. As I took Kalpana to ecstasy, all she could whisper was 'please'.

I knew exactly what she wanted. As our bodies scaled the peak of pleasure Kalpana wrapped her arms tightly around me, and our lips ravaged one another.

Euphoria was the only way to describe what we shared that night. This would be a night I would never forget.

We grabbed a blanket and spent the night together on the couch. Too soon, 6 a.m. arrived and Kalpana's alarm went off. Rushing to get our clothes and personal items, we cleaned ourselves as best we could and hurried out of the office before anyone got in.

Before leaving for our homes, we decided to stop for a cup of coffee. The two of us couldn't wipe the smiles off our faces. Kalpana told me how much she had enjoyed our night together. It was something she wouldn't ever forget. But it was also something that couldn't happen again. There were too many things in the way and in the long run it wouldn't work out.

A little disappointed, I told her I understood. I was just happy to have spent that incredible night with her and appreciated how she took care of me and didn't make me feel insecure about my inexperience.

That was the last time I ever had a conversation with Kalpana. Whenever we pass by one another in the call centre these days we say hi, but that is it. Sly smiles are the hidden ways we communicate.

The Cinema

Rajesh was just on the verge of becoming a man. Like most nineteen-year-olds he dreamed about getting out of Belapur, his small hometown where nothing exciting ever happened. He longed for the adventure and romance that he so frequently saw in films.

Belapur was a very uneventful place. Just one main road ran down the town flanked by a handful of local businesses. A couple of kirana shops, a car repairman, a small cinema, a church and two temples and a market were the main attractions.

It had its own railway station where trains stopped once a day. Behind the station was the sprawl of houses and on the other side of the railway tracks was an ancient fort where young men often hung out to smoke.

Everything about Belapur was small except for

the river. The youth of the town loved swimming in it during the summer months. The river's colours changed with the seasons and it followed the ebb and flow of the lives of the town-folk with their festivals and celebrations, and even their deaths. Apparently, souls went into the river after death.

Besides swimming and watching movies at the cinema, the young men in his town did have one other hobby. Rajesh and his friends would often sneak behind the cinema and watch dirty foreign films on their phones. The videos were very low quality and they couldn't understand much of what was going on, but when you are a horny young adult that was enough to get you off. Once they got their fill, the pack of friends would run down to the field and relieve themselves.

Rajesh was determined to leave Belapur and join the army after his studies. Most of his school friends would either join the local chemical factory or farm on their land. But defending his country was important to Rajesh and he was proud to be Indian. There wasn't anything he would miss about the town, except for a girl named Kamana.

Kamana, a girl from his neighbourhood, was the

The Cinema

most beautiful thing he had ever seen. She was the same age as Rajesh, but had a certain maturity about her that he was very attracted to.

Her name meant 'desire' which was quite appropriate since he frequently fantasized about her. But she wasn't just the object of his desires, she was also someone he pictured marrying and having a family with. She was the only person who evoked real emotion in him.

When Rajesh wasn't in college or with his friends he spent his time watching Kamana. She worked at the local tailor's, sewing clothes. He loved how determined she was at making sure every piece of clothing she touched came out just perfect. She would always smile and admire her work as if it gave her a sense of accomplishment – even when she darned a hole in a blouse.

Rajesh had a favourite spot on the roof of his neighbour's house where he would spend hours sitting and watching her do her chores or playing with her younger siblings in her walled yard.

Sometimes it seemed like Kamana knew he was watching her and was pretending she didn't. She would turn towards his direction and smile to herself slyly. Rajesh would see her expression and get flustered. He wasn't sure she was smiling at him but just the possibility made him happy.

Being a virgin, Rajesh was constantly filled with sexual desires. He often had erotic fantasies of Kamana and himself having a swim in the river that ended in him losing his virginity.

He had played out the scenario in his mind a million times. They would be standing by the edge of the river. The sun was so hot that they wanted nothing more than to shed their clothing which was completely stifling.

Rajesh starts to take off his clothes first, so Kamana would feel more comfortable. Once he has taken off his shirt, he slowly starts to unbuckle his trousers. As he steps out of his pants, their hearts start beating faster.

Now Kamana begins to get more into the moment. She turns away from Rajesh and slowly starts removing her dress. The smooth, dark skin of her back glows as it catches the brilliant sunlight. As she turns around to face Rajesh he is instantly drawn to her perky, sweet breasts that hide behind a white cotton bra.

He is hugely excited by now, and Kamana cannot

The Cinema

be in doubt of his arousal. Not saying a word, Rajesh slowly removes his underwear.

With their bodies almost touching, he leans over and kisses Kamana delicately on her lips. He wants her so badly but is also so afraid of frightening her.

Rajesh places his hands on her waist, then nervously works his way around to undo her bra. He gently and slowly removes her bra, as if afraid to touch her. A shudder of excitement runs through her as her ample breasts are set free.

She is clearly overcome with the same passion that Rajesh feels. Sweat pours off their bodies now, making them glisten in the sun.

Kamana slowly removes her panties. The slow, sliding movement of her panties down her thighs has Rajesh's heart beating fast, his body shaking.

Her untouched body too trembles with excitement as she stands there waiting for what would happen next. Rajesh grabs her hand, guiding her into the river. There is nothing between their bodies and the cool water, and it is the most emancipating experience the two have ever had.

Standing waist-deep in the water, Kamana's

perky breasts now pressed firmly against his chest, they almost become joined as one. His manhood is dangerously close to the most intimate parts of Kamana's body, yearning to enter her. As they begin to kiss passionately they use their hands to explore each other's bodies. Her dark skin is so smooth and soft, like silk on his fingertips. Kamana's fingers play with his chest hair, even as her lips cling to his.

Kissing her neck, Rajesh slowly moves his hands down Kamana's back until he reaches her voluptuous buttocks. Grabbing her buttocks with a firm yet gentle hold, he lifts her on to him.

With her legs wrapped tightly around his waist, Rajesh slowly enters Kamana. This is his first time making love, but he understands that he has to be gentle with Kamana, as a woman's first time is a different experience from a man's.

As Rajesh moves further into Kamana, she throws back her head in passion. Her eyes are closed, her hands pull at his hair, as she moans in total ecstasy. Her breasts are in Rajesh's face, and he begins to kiss them, making sure no area goes untouched by his tongue. Electric sensations course through her entire body.

With their bodies still intertwined, Rajesh carries

Kamana over to a soft grassy area by the riverbank. Laying her gently on the grass, his body on top of hers, he continues to tenderly thrust his body against her, in a sensual rhythm.

They take a moment to stare deeply into each other's eyes as their passion mounts. As their bodies near fulfilment, they start to move faster. Their slow, gentle movement, similar to the river's soft currents, now transforms into the heavy crashing of ocean waves during a storm. Kamana's hands dig into Rajesh's back, desperately clinging on to his body now dripping in sweat. The tingling sensations between her thighs grow more intense with Rajesh's each thrust. Knowing that she is close to total ecstasy, he gives her three more rapid deep thrusts.

In total euphoria, they lie there for a few minutes – bodies drained and completely drenched. Panting heavily as their heartbeats begin to calm, Rajesh looks into her eyes and tells her he loves her. Kissing his lips with a smile, Kamana tells him that she loves him too.

This was the fantasy that Rajesh played out in his head over and over. He'd hide in the field behind an old banyan tree where no one could see him. With his heart thumping and blood racing from recanting this sensual fantasy, he would touch himself until he was completely satisfied.

That fantasy was the only thing that gave Rajesh any pleasure in his small town.

One night Rajesh and his friends went to the cinema to watch a movie that was just released. Like a pack of wild dogs, they made their way down the road laughing, screaming and causing a stir as young men are wont to do. As Rajesh waited in the queue to buy tickets, he spotted Kamana standing with a group of girls. His legs nearly gave way. Was the girl of his dreams really just steps away from him?

One of Rajesh's friends recognized a few girls in the group and decided to go over and talk to them. Eager to join his friends, he gave his money to the ticket guy and made his way to the group.

Everyone spoke excitedly about the new movie they had eagerly been waiting to watch for several months. In a place like Belapur, where nothing ever happened, a new movie was a hot topic for the young men and women.

Rajesh stood there silently as his friends chattered away with the lovely girls. Their loud voices, their laughter and yelling were nothing more than background noise – all his senses were focused on Kamana.

He could smell the flowery scent of her perfume, and with every breath his heart started to beat faster. Here was his opportunity to speak with the girl he had fantasized about marrying one day, but he was frozen with fear.

As the group began to enter the cinema, Kamana walked up to Rajesh and introduced herself. In complete and utter shock, Rajesh returned the greeting and introduced himself. He had to give himself a quick pinch to make sure it wasn't some sort of daydream he was having.

That moment was very real. Rajesh had always known Kamana was beautiful, but standing in front of her he was able to take in all the small details he had never noticed before. Her eyes had a stunning hint of green in them, something very uncommon in their town. Long, thick eyelashes perfectly coated with black mascara and small crystals accenting each side. Her long, dark hair swayed from side to side when she talked, like the current from the river of his fantasies. Her skin so creamy and brown was like a delicious piece of caramel candy his mouth longed to taste.

Their friends took their seats in the theatre. Plucking all his courage, Rajesh asked Kamana if she wanted to sit with him during the movie and she eagerly agreed. It was like a romantic scene from a movie that he so desperately wanted to experience.

The two made quiet conversation as they waited for the film to start. They had just met but it felt like they had known each other for years.

As the lights started to dim, the two sat back in their seats. The movie started to play and everyone's eyes were glued to the screen, except for Rajesh. His head was facing the screen but his mind was fixated on the beauty on his right.

Twenty minutes into the movie, Rajesh noticed Kamana's hand on the armrest between them, just inches away from his hand. Slowly he too raised his hand to the rest, little by little getting closer to Kamana's hand. Beads of sweat began to form on his forehead as he attempted to place his hand on hers.

The moment had come – his hand was on hers. He waited anxiously for her response. Would she move her hand away? Would she get angry and tell him she didn't like him? A hundred different scenarios rushed

The Cinema

through Rajesh's head in that second as he waited for her response.

Kamana looked down at his hand on hers, then looked up at Rajesh and gave him a smile. Words couldn't describe the feelings that overcame Rajesh at that very moment, as if a dream had finally come true for him.

The two stayed hand in hand for the duration of the movie. As the lights came on their friends noticed the handholding and started whistling and making kissing noises. Rajesh and Kamana laughed it off and the group left the theatre.

Kamana asked Rajesh if he would walk her home. As they started making their way down the road, Kamana began to tell Rajesh where she lived, but before she could he interrupted by saying he already knew. Instantly he realized what he had said and worried that he had ruined any chance of something happening between them.

But Kamana just giggled and gave him a wink. Rajesh tried to come up with a reasonable excuse but nothing came out except a stuttering mess of words.

Kamana leaned towards Rajesh and whispered in his ear that she always knew he was watching her from

Sweet Dreams

afar. Rajesh immediately started to blush and with a sparkle in his eyes and a huge smile on his face he said that he hoped he never made her feel uncomfortable. She said that having him near her gave her a warm feeling in her heart like she was never alone.

The two made their way down the road. They sat in a little hidden area to the side of her home where they could be alone. Nestled together they sat for another hour talking about their dreams for the future. Kamana too wanted to leave their dismal town and pursue adventure in a big city.

The two began to kiss passionately. Kamana whispered in Rajesh's ear that even though they had just met she wanted him to be her first lover. She had never met anyone else as special as Rajesh and the idea of losing her virginity to him would be a special memory she would cherish for all time.

Rajesh couldn't believe what he had heard. This was the moment he had been fantasizing about for so long. But what he said took both of them by surprise. Rajesh gave her a soft kiss on her lips and said that he would love to 'be her first'. Then he told her it would happen some day, but not now. Kamana gave Rajesh a confused look.

The Cinema

He reassured Kamana that his feelings for her were the same but he wanted it to happen when he was a man. To Rajesh, it meant when he could afford to take Kamana away to a big city like they had always dreamed. This made Kamana's attraction and feelings for Rajesh grow even stronger.

The two became a couple for the next year until Rajesh finished school. Enjoying every moment that they could spend together, they explored each other's bodies, kissed, caressed and talked but never made love.

The next three years when Rajesh was away were extremely difficult for the couple. With mostly letters to keep their love alive, Kamana grew sad and lonely as the months went by. She longed for Rajesh's return, yearned for his touch but worried at the possibility that it wouldn't happen. Would Rajesh come home, would he remember their promise to each other? Had there been other women in the big city, surely there were so many who were so much more beautiful than her?

One early morning she heard loud yelling coming from inside the house as she worked in the yard. Fearing that something had happened to one of her

Sweet Dreams

family members, she ran inside with her heart racing. Rajesh had returned.

Kamana was in shock – she dropped to her knees as the tears ran down her cheeks. Rajesh walked up to her and kneeled down so he was face to face with his beautiful woman. With tears in his eyes he looked into hers and said he was home, ready to build a life in the big city with the woman he wanted to spend his entire life with. Tears of joy flooded the home – but Rajesh and Kamana heard nothing, cared for no one. They clung to each other, together forever.

The Neighbour

I have had two lives. In my early twenties, just after I had finished college, I married a young, successful businessman from Pune, my hometown. It seemed I had the perfect life, a handsome husband, a beautiful house and all the things a girl dreams about while growing up.

I didn't know that what came along with that package was a husband who was a habitual cheater. I caught him on numerous occasions and he always just cried his way back into my arms. It was my fault after the first time. Because I forgave him each time, he took it as my permission to do it again – just as long as he apologized, he was in the clear.

But after five years I had had enough. I asked for a divorce and he was more than happy to give it to me. Because he was a shrewd businessman I walked away with very little. But the peace of mind the divorce brought was worth everything to me.

My new life was quiet and even boring. I got myself a job in a large office in Mumbai. I moved into a newly built apartment complex in a nice suburb. It was the first time I'd ever lived alone, but it was fun. Being single was so foreign to me that I really didn't go out much.

As the months went by I started to get more comfortable with this life of solitude. I stopped caring about how I looked when I wasn't at work and didn't even try to venture out. Nor did I have too many friends: I had left most of them behind with the divorce.

The only thing I did for entertainment was spy on my neighbours. The apartments were laid out such that all the living rooms and bedrooms faced a central courtyard. So my living room and bedroom looked out directly on to the living rooms and bedrooms of the other flats.

The weekends were always the best for people-watching. I would turn off all the lights in my apartment, pour a glass of wine, then sit on a chair positioned by the window, behind a sheer curtain, with my dad's old birdwatching binoculars. No one could see me when the lights were turned off. I would crack open the window so I could hear the voices of my neighbours drift into my flat, and it also gave me a good view of everyone.

I saw the same episodes play themselves out in front of my eyes each week. There was an old couple who constantly bickered over what television show to watch. A teenage girl, whose parents thought she was the perfect daughter, sneaked out every weekend and came home drunk hours later with her clothes all messed up. There was a sad, lonely lady who sat on her couch sobbing for hours, I never knew why.

They were all entertaining to watch, but there was one person I was obsessed with. He was a single man who looked like a Bollywood star. He had the perfect body and would always walk around his apartment in his underwear. Every weekend he would come home in the late hours of the night with a different girl. It was always a hot twenty-year-old with perky breasts and a tight butt.

They would usually have a drink, then get right into having wild sex. I found it interesting that they always left the lights on. I guess if you looked as hot as him and the girls he slept with, you don't feel self-conscious about your body. Sometimes he would position himself right in front of the window while having sex, as if he knew someone was watching. On a few occasions he looked out, and I would fantasize that he knew it was me watching him, and he was performing to get me off.

The sex was always hard and fast. It was as if he'd get what he wanted and then send them on their way. The sex never failed to turn me on. I usually had to take a hot shower to relieve myself of the built-up sexual energy immediately after my voyeuristic act. Watching this guy was the closest I got to having a sex life. I had given up that part of myself after the divorce.

One Friday I returned home in the late evening after work, as was my habit. It had been a long week and I was especially looking forward to my weekend. I jumped into the shower to freshen up, prepared some dinner, poured myself a glass of wine, paid a few bills and did some chores around the apartment.

The evening passed and I sat down for my usual Friday night routine of neighbour-watching. Everyone was in the midst of his or her usual night rituals but my sexy neighbour wasn't home. Usually he would have

The Neighbour

brought someone home by now. Maybe he was still out on the hunt or had ended up at her place for once.

I patiently waited for him to show up but he didn't appear. It was close to midnight so I decided I would just head to bed. There would be no sexy live show for me that night – though it was exactly what I needed at the time.

As I headed to my bedroom I heard my doorbell ring. The ring startled me: no one came to my flat this late. As I looked out of the peephole I couldn't believe my eyes. It was my hot neighbour.

Trying to calm my beating heart, I asked who it was. He responded that it was Vivek, from Apartment No. 17. He said he was sorry to bother me but he had lost his keys and cellphone and that mine was the only apartment in the block with a light on. Could he come in and use my phone?

I asked him to wait a bit as I tried to calm my nerves. I ran back to my room, put on some lipstick and tried to do something sexy with my hair. As I looked at myself anxiously in the mirror, I realized with a sigh that it didn't really matter. Why was I getting dolled up for someone like him? I knew the kind of girls he was into and I was the exact opposite.

I took a deep breath, opened the door and greeted him nervously, showing him into the living room where the phone was. He sat himself down, making small talk in a relaxed way. He said he had lost his keys, wallet and phone earlier that night and had to walk home all the way from the bar he was at. He had seen me before in passing, he said with a smile. There was something about me that made him feel comfortable, and he felt sure he could intrude on me tonight.

I acted coy so I wouldn't look desperate and said I couldn't quite place him but was happy to meet him too. Of course I vividly remembered each time we had passed each other in the hall. I could even remember what he was wearing on every occasion I had seen him. But I wasn't going to tell him that.

Vivek dialled the apartment manager but no one answered. He thanked me and said he would go wait on the courtyard bench. Perhaps the security guard could help him. I told him that it was ridiculous and he could wait here as long as he needed.

Vivek looked very relieved. He walked over and sat on the chair by the window. Instantly my heart gave a lurch. I hadn't put away the binoculars and they were sitting right on the window ledge.

The Neighbour

As Vivek sat himself down he immediately noticed the binoculars. He looked up at me and gave me a naughty smile. He was surprised to see my light on this late, he said. Usually when he looked over to my apartment it was always dark with the window cracked open.

Had he worked out my secret? I lied and told him that after dinner I usually went to the study in the back of the flat to finish off my work before going to bed.

Vivek looked at me and smiled. I couldn't tell if he had bought my story. He picked up the binoculars and peered out of the window. He couldn't believe how clear the view was, he said with pretend surprise. I bet if you looked, you'd have a great view into my bedroom, he said with a wicked laugh.

I giggled and pretended that I didn't know he lived across the courtyard.

He asked if it would be a bother to have a glass of wine while he waited. I grabbed two glasses and started to pour, glad to escape from his knowing eyes. All of a sudden I felt Vivek right behind me. His warm breath on the back of my neck sent shivers down my spine. He wrapped his arms around my waist and whispered in my ear. He said that he knew

I had been watching him, and that he liked it. It wasn't a coincidence that he always had sex with the lights on and the curtains open. He wanted me to see him, and he knew that watching him turned me on. Knowing that I was turned on turned him on too.

He twirled me around so we were facing each other. I could feel his erect manhood pressing against my body. He asked me if I had ever fantasized about being one of those women he was with.

Filled with anxiety, I could not even look at his face. I was so aware of his smell, the muscles that pushed against his shirt. Every part of my body wanted him to take me right there, but I was too scared to tell him. It had been so long since I had been with a man.

He leaned towards me and I closed my eyes, aching to feel the softness of his lips make contact with mine. Instead, he whispered that it was probably best that he left. Standing there for a minute, he waited for my response, but I couldn't speak.

Vivek made his way to the door but before he let himself out, I managed to find my voice and begged him to stop. He turned around with a knowing smirk, as if he knew that I would ask him to stay, that I wouldn't be able to let him go. He walked back to me

The Neighbour

slowly. My heart was beating so fast I could barely hear his voice. I was sure my legs would give way. I was wet with longing. He asked why I wanted him to stay. In a deep, confident voice, he told me that all I had to do was tell him what I wanted, what I needed.

I was so nervous my eyes began to tear up. Gathering all my courage I looked him in the eye and asked him to take me. I wanted him to take me like he took those other women, I said. To make me feel like there was nothing else in the world he wanted more.

He took the final few steps towards me and gently stroked the sides of my face with his soft, delicate hands. Without saying a word, he moved his hands down to the top of my blouse and ripped it open in a single swift move. My breasts spilled out of my top as the buttons clattered to the floor. Vivek tossed the garment to the floor and ran his fingers across my chest, caressing my breasts and my neck. I could barely breathe. I could barely think. I wanted him so much.

I felt his hands make their way to my back and with a gentle motion he undid my bra. As he removed it, my body was awash with a feeling of freedom that I hadn't felt before. His strong hands cupped my breasts as he looked deep into my eyes. His piercing stare penetrated my deepest desires, which had been buried in my soul for long.

There was no question that in that moment my body belonged completely to him.

He bent down and placed his lips on my breasts, exploring every inch of them with his lips and tongue. My body trembled as he licked my most sensitive parts. Electrical currents seem to course through my entire being.

Vivek took my hand and walked me over to the dining table. With his strong arms he pushed everything off it in one strong swing. The sound of breaking dishes echoed through the apartment. But neither of us cared. He lifted me up and laid me on the table. With a quick pull, he removed my skirt.

Holding up my leg, he began to kiss it delicately, slowly moving towards my feminine area. He placed his fingers on the side of my panties and I could feel the lace tear against my skin as he ripped them off.

I lay there, completely nude, waiting for his next move. My eyes closed involuntarily as I began to feel his warm breath on my thighs. Blood raced through my veins, my body tense and strained with anticipation. I couldn't help but let out a moan as

I felt his soft lips on my most intimate parts. He discovered feelings that I had buried away; his hands and mouth could satisfy the animalistic urges my body desperately craved.

Vivek stood up to remove his pants. Standing at the edge of the table he pulled me up against his body. Placing one hand on my breast, the other on my waist, he entered me. His well-endowed manhood filled me with an overwhelming sensation of ecstasy.

He placed his hands around my neck and pulled me up so he could kiss my lips. At the same time, he began thrusting inside me in a steady rhythm. With each strong push my body crept closer and closer to total ecstasy.

Vivek then lifted me up off the table and stood up. My legs were wrapped tightly around him, and my hands held on to his sweaty neck. He was strong enough to carry my weight. I began to moan loudly, my head thrown back now even as my thighs clung on to him.

In his final thrusts I felt his body tighten, his heartbeat in sync with mine. His warm, heavy breathing felt like the sun's heat on my silky skin. As we climaxed our lips tasted each other, one last time.

Vivek lay on the couch, exhausted, as I made my way towards the shower in a daze. I couldn't believe what I had just experienced. It's only once in a lifetime that people's fantasies are truly fulfilled. Standing naked in front of the bathroom mirror, as I looked at myself and stroked my body, I felt sexier than I ever had before. I had been alone so long, and felt so unattractive. This beautiful man had changed all of that.

I walked back into the living room to see if Vivek wanted to have another glass of wine, but he wasn't there. As quickly as he had come into my life, he was gone even faster.

I sat down on the chair by the window. Picking up the binoculars, I trained it across the courtyard to his apartment. Vivek was standing at the window with his shirt off, drinking a beer. He smiled and waved. I smiled back and put the binoculars down.

The One

The night Raj proposed to me was the most memorable night of my entire life.

We had been dating for a little over three years. Raj owned a beautiful home in a pleasant area of Bangalore, close to his work. I had met him in university in the US in our final year. It was a whirlwind romance; we came from different cultures, but I immediately knew he was the one for me. So when we both graduated, I moved to India and got myself a job with an international NGO based out of Bangalore so I could be with him.

We both had challenging jobs and juggling our busy schedules and spending quality time was often hard. But we always made an effort, especially to go all out on romantic dates every once in a while. Our efforts usually paid off in a magical and fun way. And that night proved to be especially so.

Earlier in the day Raj had called me and said he had made reservations for dinner at one of our favourite restaurants. He told me to look under our bed where he had hidden a surprise for me. Raj was always doing little things to make me feel special and loved.

I reached down and pulled out a large, shiny black box, tied with a beautiful gold ribbon. My heart was racing as I opened the box, excited and anxious to see what he was surprising me with.

The first thing I saw inside was a small envelope with the words 'To my lovely Kiara…' The note said, 'A beautiful woman deserves a beautiful dress — Luv, Raj'.

My eyes started to tear up as I pulled out the most exquisite dress I had ever seen. It was something fit for a movie star. A form-fitting long, white dress with two sexy cut-outs around the sides. This wasn't a dress you wore at home for dinner. This was an all-eyes-on-me dress that had to be shown off at the most elegant of restaurants.

Since I had about a few hours until dinner I decided to go down to the salon to get my hair and make-up done. I had been given a beautiful dress; I had to make sure I looked amazing in it.

After the indulgent salon session, I raced home to get dressed for dinner. Raj would be home any minute and I was getting more and more excited. When I was done, I looked at my reflection in the mirror. I couldn't recognize the woman I saw. I felt utterly beautiful.

The front door opened and I heard Raj call out my name, 'Kiara, I'm home' in a funny accent. He did that every time he came home from work. It was a quirk he picked up from an American television show when we were in college together and which he thought was *so* hilarious.

Raj entered the room and stood there for a minute, just staring at me. Nervously I asked him if I looked okay. He walked up to me, grabbed my hands and told me that I was a vision of beauty, unlike anything he'd ever seen before. Instantly my eyes began to well up, a usual sign that I was about to cry. He leaned in towards me, planted a kiss on my lips and told me I had spent too much time getting ready to now mess up my make-up. We laughed — then made our way to the restaurant.

We walked into the restaurant and gave the

hostess our name. She said we were ready to be seated and asked us to follow her to the back room of the restaurant. I noticed many empty tables in the main room that might have been more suitable but didn't make anything of it.

At the door, Raj put his hand around my back and gently pushed me to go in first. I walked in to see the room full of our friends and family. Everyone was standing, laughing and looking at us with warmth and love.

I was in total shock, not to mention completely confused. It wasn't my birthday, and I couldn't fathom any other reason for everyone to be celebrating.

Dazed, I turned around to ask Raj if he knew. But before I could speak I saw him kneeling down with a small box in his hand. With tears in his eyes, Raj began to tell me how the last few years with me had been the happiest of his life.

Coming home after a long day's work just to see me smiling back at him as he walked in was the highlight of his day. He was so excited to see what the rest of our lives had in store for us. And then, in his deep, sultry voice, he asked the question I had dreamed of my entire life. He opened the little box, which contained a beautiful five-carat diamond ring, and asked if I would marry him.

I couldn't believe what was happening. Raj and the rest of the room anxiously awaited my response. Just as he started to get a little nervous, I screamed 'YES' as loud as I could. The room erupted into a cheerful roar.

We made our rounds through the entire room thanking everyone for being part of that special moment in our lives. It was great to share the night with our families and close friends. My parents had flown out especially for the evening from the US, his siblings had gathered from all over the country. The next day, Raj's parents held a traditional Indian engagement ceremony for us. It was all exactly as I had imagined.

For the next eight months we spent so much of our lives planning the perfect wedding. With Raj and me working full-time, trying to work out all the details was extremely stressful to say the least. Luckily Raj's efficient mother was there to help with everything.

But the stress was a small price to pay for the magical day that I became 'Mrs Raj Malhotra'. Dressed in a beautiful wedding dress (made in red Banarasi silk), I made my way down the aisle; with every nervous step making my way closer and closer to the man I was about to spend the rest of my life with.

Our wedding night was one of the most passionate moments we had ever shared. The wedding suite was filled with a sea of white flowers, the same flowers that were showered on us in the church. Candles covered every surface in the room and were laid out on the floor, making a pretty path to the private garden of the suite. We sat in the garden, gazing at the beautiful stars that looked like millions of diamonds shimmering in the sky.

Both of us were exhausted by the day's events, but we made sure to save just enough energy to consummate that very special night. Raj helped me out of my wedding dress slowly. The soft touch of his warm hands on my back, the slow, sexy way he unzipped my wedding dress began to turn me back to life. I loved how warm his breath felt on my skin. He began to kiss my neck, then covered my back with kisses.

Before he could completely undress me, I turned around and pushed him away. The cat and mouse game was something that always got us excited. I knew that he wanted me badly — I made sure to give it to him little by little so I could tease him into a frenzy.

The One

I asked him to remove his clothes and he obliged. I laid him on the bed and climbed on top of him. I felt his manhood throbbing against my thighs as I swayed my body back and forth. He pulled me down so my ample breasts were close enough for him to taste. His tongue covered every part of my breasts. A tingling sensation started to course through my blood. He stood up, carrying me with him, my legs wrapped around his waist. As we kissed passionately, he moved his hands down to my waist and lifted me onto him. As our bodies connected, I let out a sultry moan. He knew what my body desired, a gentle touch but a strong and forceful thrust.

We made love three times that night. It was the most passionate encounter either of us had had in our entire lives. We spent the rest of the week in our hotel room, and stayed mostly in bed. Our bodies naked, ready to be ravaged at any moment.

A few months after the wedding we began talking about the next step in our relationship — having children. We had so much love to give and it made perfect sense to share it with a baby. Despite our domesticity, we still kept our tradition of having special date nights. On those occasions Raj usually made his way home from work with wine and flowers. He loved bringing me white flowers like the ones we had from our wedding day and always wrote a special note on a little card which he would place in the arrangement.

I too would plan my surprises on these nights. This time, I had cooked up a feast for dinner, unlike anything I'd ever made before. His mother had given me a few of his favourite recipes and I knew he'd love them. Raj called that evening to let me know he'd be home in about ten minutes.

With candles lit, and the table set, I sat and waited for Raj to get home. Ten minutes went by and he wasn't home. Thirty minutes passed, still not home. I repeatedly tried calling his cell but there was no answer. After an hour I called his office to see if he had gone back to work, but no. Concerned, I called his parents, brother and cousins, but no one in his family had heard from him that day. I started to grow very worried.

I tried calling Raj's cell phone again, still no answer. Just then my phone rang. The voice on the other side said they were calling from the hospital. I instantly froze. My heart began beating loudly. It was a doctor, calling to let me know that Raj had been in a car accident.

He was crossing an intersection when a drunk driver ran a light and slammed right into the side of his car. He said the ambulance got there quickly but there wasn't anything they could do. Raj was pronounced dead at the scene. I dropped to the floor. My screams echoed through the neighbourhood like a scene from a horror film. The voice on the phone tried to console me, but I was hysterical.

The next few weeks were the worst of my life. I went through the Hindu mourning ceremonies like a zombie and slipped into a deep, dark depression. Raj's and my family tried to get me to see a therapist but I wasn't interested. Attending work was out of the question so I took a leave of absence. I pretty much isolated myself from the rest of the world. I stopped taking calls from friends and family. Even my mother and father, who had moved to Bangalore for a few months just to be with me, weren't allowed to come over.

Months went by and my condition got worse. I lost the will to live and increasingly felt that death was the only way to silence the grief. One particularly lonely night I poured myself a tall glass of wine. I sat down on my bed and emptied a bottle of sleeping pills on to a pillow. As I sipped my wine, the pills laid out in front of me began to exert a pull on me. All I could think of was wiping out the pain, once and for all. Wiping the tears from my eyes, I grabbed a handful of pills. Just as I was about to swallow them, the electricity in the house went out. I hated the dark, and dreaded the idea that I would suffer through my last hours, lying there helpless with no light.

I grabbed a lighter and started walking through the house lighting candles. As I lit the last candle in the kitchen I turned around and saw a trail of white flowers strewn through the hall. They were the same flowers that were used in our wedding. I had no idea how they got there but for some reason I wasn't scared.

I started to follow the trail of flowers. The windows were closed but there was a light breeze running through the house and my sheer nightgown floated in the air as I walked down the hall. When I reached the bedroom I looked over and saw a man lying naked in my bed. It was dark I and I couldn't make out who it was. Then I heard a deep voice saying, 'Kiara, I'm home.'

The man stood up and walked towards me. As he passed the window, the moon shone its light on his face. And just like that Raj was there, standing in front of me again.

I ran to Raj, crying a fountain of tears. Could it be true? Was he back? Wrapping my arms around him tightly, I told myself I would never let go. I was so overwhelmed I couldn't even speak.

Raj ran his fingers down my cheek, moving my chin up so I could see directly into his eyes. He whispered, 'I never left.' He placed his lips on mine, giving me a delicate, probing kiss that sent a warm, familiar feeling shooting through every vein in my body. Suddenly, my tears had stopped. My heart was racing, but it wasn't fear I felt.

He told me he couldn't stay, that tonight was our only night together. I pleaded to go with him wherever it was. Raj just leaned forward, our foreheads touching one another's, and told me it was only his time to go. He asked me not to get upset, but rather enjoy the last moment we'd ever share together.

Then he began to run his fingers slowly up my

arms, until his fingers were hooked under the straps of my nightgown. He lowered the straps, down past my arms, until they had come off and my nightgown had fallen to the floor. We started kissing each other with intense passion. It was that same intense feeling I had on our wedding day. A feeling I had begun to forget.

His scent made me come alive. I was suddenly full of fire and I couldn't get enough of him. My hands and lips were tools that I used to explore every part of his body. His dark skin was so soft and smooth. My hands were lost in the tangles of his hairy chest. His manhood was strong and proud as I teased his most intimate areas.

Raj gently laid me down on the bed. He used his tongue to trace every form, every curve of my tight bare body. As he moved downward, my body was overcome with ecstasy. His hands always knew the places of my most intimate parts that could send me to heaven.

He started moving up, cupping my face, kissing my mouth with his body on top of mine. With my legs wrapped around his firm waist, he entered me. We were one again. Each passionate thrust breathed new life into my limp body. A body that had been craving Raj's touch and slowly dying.

That night we made love for hours, but it still didn't seem like enough. My body felt pleasure that I had never experienced before. I was physically drained but at the same time I had an energy that had been missing for long.

I lay in Raj's arms, trying my hardest to stay awake, to prolong whatever time we had together. But I couldn't stop myself, and exhaustedly fell asleep in his arms.

The piercing morning sunlight woke me up. I looked around the room for Raj, but he wasn't there. I checked all the rooms in the house for some sort of sign that what happened the night before was real. There wasn't a single sign that he had been there. There were no flowers, the windows were locked. Only the candles, melted away, were a reminder of the evening.

Maybe it was just a dream. But either way it was exactly what I needed to start going back to normal. The following day I went to visit my parents. They were ecstatic to see some of my old self back again. I told them I had called the school and that I would be returning the following week.

Life was starting to get back to normal. During my second week back at school I started feeling nauseous. I made an appointment with my doctor to do a check-up. I wasn't prepared for what he told me at our meeting. I was pregnant.

I couldn't believe it. There was no way this could be possible, I said. He assured me it was. He assured me that I was a hundred per cent pregnant. At that moment I realized that Raj had given me one last surprise. Something that I would treasure for the rest of my life and help keep his memory alive. It was a beautiful boy, whom I named Raj.

The Massage

Ajeet worked as a business analyst for one of the country's premier mortgage companies.

His job was very stressful. He was directly under the company executives, and he often needed to work late and through the weekends and holidays if one of them needed something right away.

After a few years of working like this, the pace had begun to take a toll on Ajeet's twenty-seven-year-old body. His neck and back were in constant pain from sitting all day and he had massive headaches from continuously staring at the computer.

One night, on his way home, he pulled into a little plaza to get some take-out food for dinner. He waited outside while it was being packed, taking in the fresh air that his lungs desperately needed after being in a stuffy office the whole day.

While he was waiting, a woman came out of the eatery and sat on the other side of the bench he was on. Ajeet was captivated by her beautiful, brown eyes and long, silky hair.

'How's your night going?' he asked the beautiful stranger.

'Good. I'm just waiting for an order I placed for lunch,' said the woman.

Ajeet laughed. 'Lunch? It's almost eight. I think you're a little late for lunch!'

'Nope, I'm right on time. I work the late shift at the massage parlour a few shops down,' she said with a grin.

Ajeet was a little shocked. He had never been to a massage parlour before but he pictured it as a seedy place with 'dirty-looking girls'. Before he could ask her more, a man from the restaurant came out and handed her a package of food.

'Well, back to work. It was nice meeting you. If you ever need to relieve some stress you know where to find me…' she said in a flirty voice as she walked off.

That night, Ajeet couldn't get the mystery woman's face out of his head. She was like no one he had ever seen before, except the heroines in his favourite

The Massage

Bollywood films. He tried to imagine what she looked like under her uniform. He pictured her with medium-sized breasts that were so high and pointed that she didn't need to wear a bra, and a firm and round butt. After lying in bed fantasizing about the woman all night, Ajeet pleasured himself before going to sleep.

The following day at work he could barely get his thoughts straight. He was groggy from lack of sleep – his vivid fantasies had kept him up nearly all night. He had a deadline approaching for an important report but she was all he could think about.

That evening, he pulled into the parking lot of the massage parlour. He sat in his car for nearly half an hour, trying to get the courage to walk in. His hand actually touched the car door a few times but his nerves got the better of him. He finally started the car and drove home.

The following three nights ended in exactly the same way. Each night Ajeet drove home without getting any satisfaction. Each night he fantasized himself to sleep, dreaming about a woman he was too intimidated to talk to.

Friday night came along and Ajeet decided to stop by a local bar on the way home. He figured a few drinks would give him the encouragement he needed to walk in and talk to his mystery woman. As some liquid courage kicked in, he decided it was time to go all the way.

When he walked into the massage parlour, a beautiful older woman greeted him at the reception and asked what type of massage he was looking for.

Ajeet had no idea what to say. He had never been to a massage parlour before and hadn't even realized you could get different types of massages. He told the receptionist he was looking for a particular woman to give him a massage. He didn't know her name but could describe her. However, what he said was so vague that the receptionist couldn't help.

Many women fit that description, she told him.

Ajeet's courage was beginning to disappear. He told the woman he had made a mistake and turned around to leave. Just as he was walking out, a door opened from behind the reception. It was her.

'Hey, I remember you...are you leaving?' she asked.

'No, no. Actually, I just got here. I was hoping to find you but realized it was tough as I didn't know your name,' Ajeet said.

'It's Priya, and I just got back from my break so if

The Massage

you're ready, we can go in now,' she told him with a sexy, welcoming smile.

The room was small, with only a massage table and a few shelves full of candles, oils and towels. Priya pulled down a few towels and put on some relaxing music. She said she would be back in a few minutes and asked Ajeet to remove all of his clothing and lie down on the table, and use the towel to cover himself from the waist down.

'All my clothes? Even my underwear?' asked Ajeet.

Priya giggled and said, 'Of course, silly, haven't you ever had a massage before?'

'Well, not really. I had someone rub my shoulders once but I was completely dressed…' he replied.

The two had a good laugh when he said this, helping ease Ajeet's nervousness.

He began removing his clothes. His fingers trembled as he proceeded to unbutton his shirt. Looking around to check that he was alone, he pulled down his pants. Ajeet had never been naked outside his home so removing his underwear made him terribly shy. He grabbed the towel and covered his manhood, then quickly pulled down his underwear and jumped on to the table.

A few minutes later, Priya walked back in. She lit a few candles and turned off the lights. The ambience of the room was very relaxing. Ajeet shut his eyes and submerged himself in the tranquil music and the warmth of the candles.

As Priya began slowly pouring massage oil on Ajeet's back, its heat started making the blood rush through his body.

He could feel Priya's soft hands as she spread the oil around his neck and all over his back. Her touch was both delicate and sure. Her strokes became more forceful as she worked the muscles in Ajeet's shoulders, undoing all the knots. In that moment, all of his tension dissolved and he forgot the stress of his job.

Then Priya began massaging Ajeet's thighs. With each firm squeeze, Ajeet's body trembled in pleasure. Her sensual touch was so exhilarating that he couldn't help getting aroused. He began to worry that she would find out.

'I don't think I was able to fully ease out the tension in your neck. Do you mind if I get on your back so I can use all my strength to work it out?' she asked.

Nervously, Ajeet agreed. He was feeling both deeply relaxed and increasingly turned on.

The Massage

Priya climbed on to the massage table, sitting on Ajeet's buttocks with her legs on either side of him. She leaned forward and began to work her fingers deep into the tense muscles in his shoulders. As she massaged him, Ajeet felt something on his back. It was a warm, tickling sensation that was pleasurable, but he couldn't figure out what it was. He was too relaxed to ask so he just lay there enjoying her work.

Priya finally asked him to turn over so she could work on his chest. Ajeet's heart stopped. He was still fully erect and knew there would be no hiding it if he turned around.

'You know, I think we're good. I feel totally relaxed. This is the first time I have had a massage so I think I better take it a little easy,' he told her.

Priya was confused. 'But we're not done, it's important to work out the muscles in your chest. Am I not doing a good job?'

Now Ajeet felt bad – he didn't want her to think he was stopping because she was below par. 'It's not that at all, I'm just a little embarrassed to say why,' Ajeet said shyly.

'What is it? You don't have to feel embarrassed

with me. I'm a professional. But not only that…I…I like you,' she replied.

He hesitated at first but then rolled over.

As Ajeet turned around, he realized that the sensation he had felt on his back were Priya's breasts rubbing against him. She had been massaging him completely naked. This made him even harder.

Even with the towel covering his waist it was very apparent that he was aroused. He lay there awkwardly, waiting to see her reaction. Priya just smiled. 'Is that all? It's completely natural for that to happen during massages,' she told him in a soft voice. 'Please don't feel embarrassed.'

She had a way of making him feel very comfortable. Ajeet closed his eyes and gave in, waiting for Priya to continue her magic. As the sticky massage oil dripped on his chest, Ajeet's breathing became very deep. He could feel his heartbeat slowing down as she slathered the oil on to his smooth chest. Every muscle in his body felt relaxed.

In his mind he kept picturing Priya's nude body rubbing against his own. He couldn't help but open his eyes to make sure he wasn't imagining it. Priya's beautiful, big, bare breasts were swaying from side to

The Massage

side as she tirelessly massaged his chest. Her skin was glowing from the sweat of her exertions.

Their eyes connected, and it felt like they were both in another world in another time. He knew that she also felt the same way. As they stared into each other's eyes Priya started to work her hands down Ajeet's chest to his stomach and his sides. With each rub of her hands he became more fixated on her firm, young body and her hands, which were now so near his manhood.

Priya grabbed the edge of the towel and slowly started to remove it. The warm air that hit his manhood felt exhilarating. He was achingly hard now.

His body filled with ecstasy as Priya began to massage his most private parts. He couldn't help but grip her smooth, nude self while she worked. His fingers began to explore her, caressing her neck, moving between her big breasts down to her stomach. She gasped as he touched her breasts, tracing out their roundness, cupping and squeezing them.

Without saying a word, Priya positioned herself right over Ajeet's firm manhood. He could feel the warmth of her flesh as she lowered herself on to him.

Priya began moving her body in a slow, circular

motion. She was moaning loudly now, overcome with pleasure. The sensual rhythm of their bodies grew faster and faster. Ajeet gripped Priya's thighs tightly and began thrusting himself against her. With each powerful thrust, they inched closer to climax.

As the two reached the final throes of their passion, Ajeet lay there with his heart racing. He could not believe how good his body felt. He was deeply relaxed and satisfied. It was a sensation he would never forget.

Ajeet never returned to the massage parlour. He thought that going back would take the fire out of his memory. On occasion he would spot Priya outside the restaurant they had first met while waiting for food. They would chat and catch up on life. The sexual encounter they had shared had created a friendship between the two.

Sometimes the thing you needed the most in life was the very thing you never would have guessed.

Rekindled Romance

After ten years of marriage the spark between my husband and me had started to fizzle out. We were only in our mid-thirties but we acted like we were in our sixties. Confession time – in the past year Ritvik and I had been intimate with each other only a handful of times.

I still loved him and I knew he still loved me but somewhere along the line we had stopped connecting with each other sexually. The shift in our relationship had started after our second child was born. We were very happy that he had come into our world but it brought a lot more stress into our relationship – our conversations were about maids, schools and doctor visits rather than about us.

One day I was feeling particularly romantic. I had spent the past few days reading a sultry, erotic novel that had reminded me of what it was like to feel sexy. I asked my mother if the kids could spend the night at her house. She agreed happily so I packed their bags and sent them on their way.

I spent the rest of the day putting myself together. I curled my hair, went for a manicure and did my make-up to perfection. In my closet was a short, black dress I hadn't worn in years. To my pleasant surprise it still fit me.

I arranged the house beautifully. The dinner table looked like something out of a magazine. Candles set the ambience of the room. I made two elegant place settings across from each other and placed a centrepiece of beautiful newly bloomed roses. It was breathtaking. The cook and the servant were given the evening off so we could truly enjoy this night privately.

When Ritvik came home, he threw his briefcase and coat on to the couch. He walked into the kitchen, right past the beautifully arranged dining room, and began telling me about an issue he had had at work that day. Clearing my throat, I nodded my head in the direction of the dining room.

Ritvik turned around and saw the candlelit room with the roses in bloom. Surprised, he asked what the occasion was. I told him I just wanted to have a romantic dinner with my husband. The kids were gone and it would be just the two of us. His eyes lit up and he walked over and gave me a kiss.

Ritvik sat at the table and poured us both a glass of wine. As I made my way to the table with our dinner, he complimented me on how beautiful I looked. FINALLY, he had noticed the effort I'd made to look good for him. We sat together and enjoyed the meal; it was great to have a peaceful dinner with each other and catch up on our lives.

After dinner I cleared the table and went to the kitchen to rinse the dishes. Ritvik walked up to the sink, wrapped his arms around me and kissed my cheek, thanking me for a wonderful meal.

I felt like the spark between us was slowly coming back. After sharing a bottle of wine and listening to his sweet remarks, my body was really in the mood for some intimacy. I asked Ritvik to get into bed, saying I'd be up in just a few minutes. With his arms still around me, he gave me a quick squeeze and said he would be waiting.

Making my way upstairs to the bedroom, I stopped at the mirror to make sure I still looked good. I walked into the room with a sexy strut, only to see Ritvik in bed, ASLEEP. Initially I thought he was just teasing me, so I walked over and removed my dress. Wearing only a new black satin bra and panties, I climbed into bed and gave him a kiss. He didn't respond so I whispered passionately in his ear that I wanted to make love.

Ritvik turned on to his side, sleepily mumbled 'good night' and began to snore lightly. I couldn't believe it! After everything I had done that night – he was asleep? I shoved him so hard, he almost fell off the bed.

Looking dazed, he asked me what was going on. I took my pillow and hit him in the face. The man I was married to didn't find me attractive any more. That was what was going on. I had never felt so unattractive in my life.

Seeing how upset I was, Ritvik apologized and said that he was appreciative of everything I had done that night. But he had had a really stressful day and was exhausted. But I knew it was more than that.

I grabbed my pillow and blanket and stormed out of the room. Making myself a little bed on the couch, I poured myself another glass of wine and lay there and cried. My marriage had dried up in front of my eyes – if it stayed this way, I knew it had no chance of lasting more than a few years. I was a romantic woman and couldn't live in a businesslike arrangement where he brought home the money and I looked after the home and the children. Many marriages may have survived like that but I wanted much, much more.

Ritvik came downstairs and saw me lying distraught. He stood there watching me but didn't offer any comforting words. Instead, he disappeared upstairs. Sometime later, he came down again and gently asked me to get ready. I was in no mood to heed his words and was irritated by his demands. But he kissed me, stroked my hair away from my face and told me to just put my dress back on and pack a light overnight bag. I hesitated, but he asked me to trust him.

I went up and came back downstairs with my dress on and my make-up touched up. I was intrigued by this new development. We jumped into the car and drove into the night. Ritvik held my hand the entire way. It was a small gesture but it warmed my heart in a way nothing had in a long time.

Sweet Dreams

We pulled into the driveway of a luxurious five-star hotel. A reservation had already been made for us. Ritvik asked me to go ahead and wait for him in the room. A beautiful bouquet of flowers was waiting for me as I walked in, alongside a bottle of champagne.

I was beginning to feel really excited when I received a text from Ritvik saying that he was sorry but he had to run down to the office for something urgent. He suggested that I go down to the hotel bar where he would join me shortly. He was doing it again! I suppressed my anger and went downstairs to wait for him.

The bar was beautiful, with huge, white pillars that were decorated with 14 carat gold detailing. As beautiful as it was I still couldn't get my mind off Ritvik and our unravelling marriage. After waiting for about twenty minutes I got a text from him saying that he would be at the office all night because of a huge crisis. He was terribly sorry and would make it up to me later. I couldn't believe it – I had now been stood up by my husband twice in a single night.

I gulped down my drink and started getting ready to head back to the room. Before I could get off the bar stool, a man walked up to me and asked if the seat next to me was taken. Just as I was about to tell him I was married, I looked up and saw that it was Ritvik. Except, he looked different than he normally did. His hair was slicked back with gel, and he was wearing an expensive shirt that wasn't buttoned all the way up. He said he hoped he wasn't being too forward but I looked so beautiful that he had to buy me a drink.

He said his name was Hari and asked me for mine. My heart was racing. I didn't understand this game but I was liking it. I told him my name was Nari and that I was very upset because I had been stood up by my husband. I was feeling lonely and was looking for a male companion. Hari sat down and we ordered a few drinks.

'So tell me about yourself,' said Hari, looking deep into my eyes. I could smell his aftershave and feel the strength of his body up close. This man didn't seem like my husband. I began to talk about myself and realized I was flirting with this handsome man. It didn't hurt that Hari made sure our glasses were constantly refilled.

The more we talked, the more excited I got. It was as if our words were saying one thing, our bodies another. Soon we were leaning close into each other, smiling and laughing. His thighs were touching mine and our arms were inching towards each other. I found myself brushing his chest accidentally as I laughed over a joke. At one point he leaned over and brushed away a lock of hair that had fallen over my face. Electricity was coursing through my body.

After a few drinks I asked Hari if he would escort me back to my room. He paid the cheque and, taking my arm, led me to the elevator. The sexual tension between us was now so strong I couldn't breathe. I invited him in to have a nightcap, wanting this night to last forever.

The hotel room looked beautiful. The lights were low and the curtains were pulled open so you could see the twinkling lights of Mumbai down below. Hari poured out two glasses of champagne for us and put on some music. He looked at me with warm, dark eyes and asked me to dance.

We danced slowly, his hands caressing my nape and mine holding his waist. And we talked. 'Tell me about your fantasies,' I found myself asking him. I had always been too shy to ask Ritvik such a question but I felt I could ask Hari anything. We talked about the wildest nights we had had as young adults, the naughtiest places we'd ever had sex, and what our deepest fantasies were.

At one point I told Hari that I was married and that it wasn't really appropriate that I was with another man in my hotel room. He looked at me and said that my husband deserved it. He was a fool for letting me out of his sight. He leaned close to kiss me. I had been waiting for that kiss for a long time and I returned it with equal passion. We stood there, in the hotel room, locked in each other's embrace.

Breaking away from the kiss, I walked to the bathroom and asked him to join me in a few minutes. I turned on the shower and removed my clothes. The steam from the hot water made my skin glow. I felt completely alive. Hari entered the bathroom nude. He looked so sexy, with his broad chest, strong legs and his manhood standing at attention.

In the shower, he rubbed his strong hands all over my big, round breasts. Our lips tasted each other as I felt him pressed against my wet body. My blood raced as his fingers began exploring me all over.

I soaked a washrag liberally with soap and began to scrub him. My fingers were lost in his chest hair, feeling the muscles in his chest and his forearms. As I made my way down, his breathing became heavy. I could feel him pulsating in my hand.

Hari took the washrag from me and poured soap all over my breasts. The sensation of the liquid against my skin was so erotic. As he lathered my breasts with soap the suds travelled down to my feminine parts. He took the cloth and gently washed the most delicate parts of my body. I trembled as his fingers discovered my most pleasurable areas.

After about twenty minutes in the shower, teasing and worshipping each other's bodies, we dried ourselves and made our way to the bed. As I lay down with Hari's naked body hovering over mine, he began kissing and licking my breasts. Tingling sensations ran throughout my body as his lips and tongue travelled down to my most intimate areas. I couldn't help but moan as I felt the warmth of his tongue moving in a circular motion around my flesh.

Hari sat me up and pulled my body against his. He made me sit on his lap. My legs were wrapped tightly around his waist and my breasts pressed against his chest. He pulled my hair back and passionately kissed my lips as my fingers dug into his back.

My heart began racing with adrenaline as I waited for him to enter me. All I wanted now was for him to be inside me. Every muscle in my body tightened as I felt Hari penetrate my body. Slowly, we merged into one. As I leaned back, his fingers gently traced the arch of my back. His rhythm increased as our bodies moved like the steady waves of the ocean.

He lowered me off him and stood up, carrying me. He turned me around so my breasts were against the cool surface of the wall. I could feel his warm breath behind my neck as he re-entered me. The feeling of his hard body pushed up against mine while I was pinned to the wall was one of the most erotic experiences I had ever had. I felt I was his toy and pleasing him was the only way to satisfy myself.

With each thrust of Hari's my body trembled with bliss. His hands held on tightly to my waist as our bodies swayed back and forth. Hari repositioned me so I was facing him. Firmly gripping my breasts, he began to thrust harder and faster. We stood there, my back against the wall, his sweaty body pinned against mine, ravaging my intimate parts. With his final few thrusts, we both reached ecstasy and collapsed.

Our bodies were limp from exhaustion as we lay on

the bed, waiting for our heartbeats to calm down. It had been so long since passion had pulsated through our veins like it did that night. We fell asleep naked, my head on Hari's chest and his arm wrapped tightly around me. As we drifted off, he whispered in my ear that my husband was very lucky to have such a special woman as his wife.

The Gardener

Last summer my husband, Kabir, hired a worker to help get our yard renovated. We had money and a big, stylish house in one of the nicest suburbs of Toronto, but he was always cheap. When it came to doing work around the house, he preferred paying slave wages to a local college kid desperate for money.

One of our neighbours referred Arjun to him. They said he was a hard worker who would come cheap and never complain. This was exactly what Kabir was looking for.

Arjun started the following week. His job was to paint the fence, pull out weeds and replant the entire yard. That was a lot of work, and probably required three or four men, but Kabir didn't want to spend much money.

One day I walked into the kitchen to pour myself a

glass of wine. As I passed by the window I saw Arjun working in the yard. He was drenched in sweat. The summer sun was unbearably hot that day and I felt bad that he was forced to endure it.

Worried he was going to pass out from the heat, I decided to get him something refreshing. I sliced up a few lemons and threw them in a large pitcher of ice water.

As I was grabbing a glass, I peeked out of the window and saw Arjun acting a little oddly. He kept looking around him as if to check if he was being watched. It seemed as if he was going to do something a little secretive. This sparked my interest.

Hiding behind the sheer curtains in the kitchen, I watched him curiously. Before too long, Arjun had pulled his shirt over his head and flung it to the ground.

The sight of his firm, muscular nineteen-year-old body covered in sweat had me instantly flustered. It had been a long time since my eyes had gazed upon such a beautiful, hard body. I had been married to Kabir in India over twenty-five years ago. I had never known another man apart from him. I often wondered what it would be like to sleep with someone else and

The Gardener

today these feelings sprang up in me again. I sat at the window for about fifteen minutes, watching the handsome young man work away in the hot sun. The sweat dripping down his torso ran in rivulets through every flexed muscle, emphasizing his beautiful body.

I'd be lying if I said I wasn't completely turned on.

Kabir walked into the kitchen and asked what I was staring at. Immediately, I composed myself and told him that I felt bad for the young man outside and was going to get him some water.

'Well, take it to him now, I don't want him dying in my yard,' Kabir replied in a harsh tone.

I made my way outside with the pitcher and a bowl of fresh mango slices. Arjun was working with his back towards me, and the view from the back was just as delicious as the front.

I quietly stood behind him for a moment, taking in his sexy, musky scent. The smell of a sweating man working with his body is so erotic. I could've stood there for hours.

I leaned closer and seductively whispered in his ear, 'Hot?' Like a scared cat, he turned and jumped in the air, knocking the pitcher of water out of my hands and drenching me.

Arjun's face turned white as a ghost, no doubt fearing his little mishap might have cost him his job. With a trembling voice, he blurted out, 'I'm so sorry, Mrs. Singh, did I get you wet?'

I pulled down my sunglasses so he could see my eyes and with a flirtatious smirk, I said, 'You have no idea…' His cheeks turned as red as a strawberry at my remark. There was something about his innocence that I found very attractive.

I told him there was more water on the patio table and to help himself. As I made my way back to the house, I could feel his stare penetrating my body. That brief encounter ignited a fire in my body.

That evening, I couldn't wait for Kabir to come to bed. I couldn't remember the last time I had actually wanted to make love to my husband, but I couldn't get the vision of Arjun's hard, sweaty body out of my head. I needed to relieve the sexual frustration coursing through my body.

When Kabir entered the bedroom I looked amazing. I greeted him wearing a long, black, sheer nightgown that barely covered my most intimate parts. A high slit on one side showed off a long, firm leg, freshly slathered with expensive lotion.

The Gardener

My sex appeal went unnoticed. Kabir walked over to me, kissed my forehead and then started off about a business deal that had gone bad, opening and closing cupboards distractedly. I sat on the bed in a provocative position, hoping to get his attention. But he couldn't be bothered with me. Packing a bag, he told me he was heading to our small flat in the city so he could beat the morning rush-hour traffic. Then he left. My night ended with a bottle of wine, a cold shower, and me crying myself to sleep.

The next day, I decided to take advantage of the hot summer weather and did some sunbathing in the yard. I think a part of me just wanted an excuse to be outside so I could watch Arjun work.

I looked sexy, wearing a one-piece bathing suit that had sheer revealing cutouts in the chest and sides. It was really more lingerie than swimsuit and was probably a style designed for a girl in her twenties. But it suited my gym-toned body just perfectly. Being a woman in her forties didn't mean I couldn't look or feel sexy.

With my hair pulled back into a tight ponytail and large gold hoops swaying from my ears, I walked outside. The black satin wrap on my shoulders floated behind me in the gentle breeze. Large, expensive sunglasses masked the lust in my eyes as I admired Arjun's firm body.

I sat myself on the lounger with a glass of wine, getting comfortable. He looked towards me and delivered a cute little smile. I waved back flirtatiously.

Gently squeezing the bottle of sunscreen onto my hand, I began to apply it to my body. Using long, slow strokes, I rubbed the sunscreen all around my arms. I applied it all over my legs, lifting them up to make sure I didn't miss a spot. Almost every inch of my smooth body was slathered up.

I called to Arjun so I could get his assistance. 'I hate to bother you, but would you mind just putting a little sunscreen on my back?' I said in a husky voice.

His eyes opened wide and his face went pale.

'Of course, ma'am,' he murmured softly.

I hated that he called me 'ma'am' – it made me sound like some old grandma. But I thanked him and handed him the bottle of sunscreen. I rolled over on the lounger so my back was towards Arjun. My swimsuit was cut low, exposing my entire back. Thirty seconds went by and nothing happened. I jokingly asked if he was still there.

The Gardener

Arjun let out a small, nervous laugh and apologized. I heard him fumbling around trying to open the bottle, eventually getting the top off. He gave it a gentle squeeze but nothing came out. He tried again, still nothing. Starting to get frustrated, he shook the bottle, pointed it at my back and gave one last forceful squeeze. I let out a loud gasp as I felt a giant, cool glob of sunscreen splatter across my back.

I turned my head around in shock, and as our eyes made contact we both burst into laughter. He took off his shirt and wiped off the excess sunscreen.

That moment broke down the invisible wall that stood between us. He began to rub the sunscreen around my back. The touch of his rough fingers against my smooth skin was exhilarating. For someone so young and nervous, he had a very commanding yet gentle touch.

I thanked Arjun and spent the next hour relaxing on the lounger, secretly watching his every move. Something about him made my blood pulsate.

I spent that night alone again. My husband's trips to the city had become increasingly frequent in the past few years. I felt like I was always alone. Even when Kabir was here, he wasn't really present. I thought I had got used to it – TV and a bottle of wine usually did the job – but today I really felt the weight of my solitude. Something had changed in me. I knew I was at breaking point and needed something more than a bottle of wine and a cold shower to get me through the lonely night.

The following morning, Kabir called to let me know he was going to stay the next three nights in the city. Part of me thought he was really doing all he could to sort out the work crisis. The other part of me knew the truth, that he was probably having an affair with some twenty-one-year-old cocktail waitress. I hoped I was wrong.

I sat in the kitchen, drinking my morning coffee, trying to calm my emotions. I was feeling angry, lonely and stressed. Then I noticed Arjun working in the yard. Something about watching him work sent a warm sensation through my body.

After about ten minutes he looked over and saw me through the window. I waved hello coyly. He looked at me and just smiled.

Friday had come and Kabir was still in the city. He asked me to go into his home office and grab some money from the safe to pay Arjun for his first week.

The Gardener

At the end of the day, Arjun approached me in the kitchen to let me know he had completed his work and that he was set to leave. I asked him to give me a few minutes to go and get his payment.

When I didn't show up, Arjun began to wander around the house looking for me. That's what I had been waiting for. Finally, I heard a soft knock on my bedroom door, followed by a nervous voice saying, 'Mrs. Singh, are you here?' I opened the door wearing a white lace negligee. My breasts looked beautiful, pushed up and perky. I had on my sexiest high-heeled shoes that accentuated the length of my legs. I felt delicious and excited.

Immediately, Arjun turned around and apologized for intruding. He offered to get his payment next week. I told him not to be silly, and to sit down on the bed while I finished getting ready.

He sat there on the edge of the bed like a nervous kitten, his hands under his thighs and his brown eyes wide open. I asked if I made him nervous. With his eyes looking at the ceiling, he said that he did feel nervous around me.

He admitted that there were times when he looked at me in an inappropriate way.

Amused, I asked him what he meant by 'inappropriate'. I was loving the effect I had on him. It made me feel strong and sexy.

'Well, I've just noticed your…like you are…I mean I've never seen a woman like you before…,' Arjun said, as drops of sweat started to form on his forehead. 'You are very attractive and sometimes I find it hard not to look at you.'

His innocence and kindness was so refreshing. I couldn't recall the last time I had felt truly attractive to someone. Maybe it was my insecurity about getting older, or maybe it was Kabir's decreasing efforts to tell me how beautiful I was.

Walking up to him, I took my finger under his chin and lifted it up. 'You never have to feel nervous around me,' I said in a flirtatious tone. He smiled and his cheeks turned bright red.

I asked him to tell me a little more about his personal life. His family, hobbies, what he liked to do with his friends. As he began to talk haltingly, I started rubbing a body lotion on my legs. It was an expensive one that I had purchased during a trip to Dubai. The scent was designed to attract men, and it gave the skin a soft, metallic sheen.

The Gardener

Arjun moved his hands on to his lap, desperately trying to conceal his growing manhood. His breathing grew heavy. 'Have you ever been with a woman before, in a sexual manner?' I asked in a soft, sultry voice.

Shocked that I would ask him such a question, he sat there frozen with fear. 'No, ma'am,' he replied in a loud whisper, followed by a gulp. 'But I have seen a naked woman before…in, uh…in a magazine…'

I leaned back against the vanity behind me, positioning my body to enhance my natural curves. Arjun could barely make eye contact with me now, and kept stealing glances at my legs, glowing softly with the lotion.

'Would you like to touch them?' I said to him, my right hand gently caressing my thigh.

Arjun didn't respond but I knew that he wanted to. I stood up and walked towards him, my body just inches from his. He looked at me, so nervous his eyes starting to water. I took his hands and placed them on the backs of my thighs. With my hands on top of his, I began to move them up and down.

The contrast of his rough hands against my silky skin felt incredible. As I moved his hands up towards my ass I could feel his fingers gripping me tighter. I let go of his hands but he continued to rub my thighs.

His inexperienced touch turned me on in a way I had never felt before. I could feel myself getting moist as his long fingers began to grow more curious.

Gathering his courage, his fingers moved upwards as he began tracing the contours of my cleavage. Looking up at me with his puppy-dog eyes, he asked, 'Can I please see them?'

Without saying a word, I took my thumbs and placed them under the straps of the negligee. Slowly, I began to move the straps down towards my shoulders. As the straps started to fall I placed my arm under my breasts, preventing the sexy garment from falling to the floor.

It seemed like every second that I teased was torture to Arjun. Biting his tongue in anticipation, he sat there waiting for me to reveal my breasts to him.

Finally, I moved my arm, letting the cool, silken material fall gently down my body until it fell to the floor. Raising my arms up, I lifted my long, dark hair to the top of my head, giving him a perfect view of my ample breasts.

Arjun's mouth dropped open. He looked at my breasts like he was admiring a fine piece of art. I took my hand and placed it behind his neck, a firm grip to let him know that I was in charge. I pulled his face towards my breasts; his warm, deep breath on my skin felt like sunlight on a hot summer day.

I placed his hands on my breasts. His trembling, caressing fingers sent shivers throughout my entire body. He delicately squeezed my breasts, releasing the pressure only to squeeze them again. Then he began to slowly trace gentle circles around my breasts. His slow exploration of my body felt both innocent and erotic at the same time. And it was taking me to the very edge.

Reaching down, I pulled his shirt over his head. I leaned closer and kissed his soft lips. As much as I wanted to take this further, I knew it was best that we saved some mystery. I whispered a thank you in his ear and handed him an envelope with the payment.

The little encounter between Arjun and me breathed new life into my soul. I suddenly felt ten years younger, I felt attractive again. More than just an object of lust, he made me feel beautiful.

The chemistry between us grew stronger over the

next few weeks. When Kabir was in the house, Arjun and I barely said a word to each other. We didn't have to, we communicated through discreet looks and gestures. Every day Arjun would leave me a beautiful flower on the doorstep in front of the patio. He had a very kind and beautiful heart.

I remember one time Kabir and I were sitting out on the patio. He was reading a magazine and I was enjoying a glass of wine. Arjun was working in the yard not too far away from us.

His body glistened from the sunlight like little gold flakes. The glass of wine had relaxed me and seeing Arjun's hot, sweaty body I couldn't help but get turned on.

I could see Arjun discreetly watching me as he did his work. With Kabir's face behind the paper, I started to flirt dangerously with him. Pulling my skirt up to my thighs I began to gently open and close my legs, like the flutter of a butterfly's wings. I casually took my finger and ran it down my chest, opening my blouse just enough for Arjun to catch a quick glance of my cleavage.

The fear of Kabir catching us made flirting even more thrilling. We played these dangerous games for

The Gardener

the next few weeks. Naively ignoring the possibility of getting caught, we began pushing the limit further and further. It got sexier as the stakes got higher.

One day Kabir had left to go to the bank. As soon as his car pulled away I walked outside and told Arjun that there was a problem with the showerhead in my bathroom. He smiled and said he would be there in a few minutes.

Arjun opened the bathroom door and a cloud of steam came out at him. I was leaning against the sink with my hair up, wearing nothing but a short satin bathrobe that was loosely tied.

'Everything here looks in good working order to me,' he said to me as he ran his finger down my chest.

'Maybe you should take out your tool and just make sure everything is good,' I whispered back.

Arjun walked up to me, taking off his shirt and tossing it to the floor. Our bodies clung to each other as we kissed urgently. Kabir could be back any minute. Arjun grabbed my waist and lifted me on to the counter, my legs wrapped around his waist. Then he unbuttoned his trousers, leaving them still on, and pulled out his fully erect manhood. My fingernails dug into the back of his neck as he entered me.

The mirror behind us started to rattle as he thrust his sweaty body against mine. His rhythm picked up and our bodies were soon overcome with euphoria. I let out a deep moan as he gave three final thrusts. Just then we heard the front door unlock. Arjun kissed me, grabbed his shirt and ran out to the yard. That was the closest we had ever been to being caught, but even then there wasn't fear.

One afternoon while Kabir was watching a cricket match in the study, I called Arjun over to the kitchen to help me open a jar. As soon as he walked in I grabbed him and gave him a passionate kiss. He grabbed my breasts and started to kiss my neck. As my hands explored his body I could feel his manhood growing.

I dragged him into my bedroom and we started to fool around. Kabir only came into our room at night so I knew we were safe there. Our hands and lips were all over each other.

Things were going great until Kabir decided he was ready for lunch. He wandered through the house looking for me and walked into our room and saw us together – my legs wrapped around Arjun's waist, and his hands in my blouse.

The Gardener

Kabir pulled Arjun off me and started to get rough with him. Arjun, now angry, charged at Kabir, slamming him into the wall. I saw him pick up a metal sculpture from the table, holding it above his head, ready to strike Kabir, and screamed for him to stop.

Kabir, lying on the floor in pain, told him to get out of his house. 'If I ever see your face again, you're a dead man,' he shouted in a broken voice.

Arjun looked over and saw me hysterical, crying, on the floor. Black lines from my mascara ran down my cheeks. Taking my hands, he asked if I was okay. Barely able to speak, I asked him to leave.

'You can't stay here with this man. I'm not leaving without you,' shouted Arjun as he attempted to pull me up to leave with him.

I resisted, pleading with him to leave. 'Please, Arjun, you're only making things worse. I'll be okay but you have to leave now.'

Kabir kept yelling obscenities as Arjun stood there staring down at me. His eyes filled with tears. I looked up with tears falling down my face and begged him one more time, 'Please go…'

He took my hand in his, brought it to his mouth

and gave it a soft kiss. As he walked away I could feel my heart shattering into a thousand pieces.

The next few months were rough. Kabir was full of anger and my heart was full of pain at what I had lost. But eventually things in our household went back to normal. I continued to float through life as a lonely, lost flower. Just an object my husband treasured but never appreciated.

One day I heard a knock at the door. When I opened it, no one was there. I looked around and didn't see anyone. As I was about to close the door I looked down and saw a single white flower lying on the ground. It was the same flower that Arjun used to bring me every day.

Moon

Diya spent her days working in her mother's small tailoring shop. Her job was to organize the work, collect payments and handle clients.

The days were long and tiring. The monotony of the job drove Diya mad, and she longed for a bit of excitement in her life. She felt lonely and restless. A few years ago, she'd had a boyfriend who had treated her badly. Their marriage had been finalized but it had all gone very wrong. Not only was she left with bruises on her body but her heart, too, was bruised to numbness. Since then Diya hadn't been able to trust any man. If anyone showed an interest in her, she ran in the other direction. But secretly she couldn't help longing for love.

At night she would look out of her window and stare at the moon. When she was a young girl, her mother had told her that the moon had special powers and would grant wishes to those in need. Now, longing to find someone she could share her heart with, she began making a wish to the moon.

Every night it was the same wish.

Dear Moon,

I stand here looking up at you, asking if you could grant me one wish. I don't want money or fame or success. But I wish for a man in my life.

Not just any man, but a man who is good to me. Whose touch can keep me warm on the coldest of nights. Someone whose smile is as bright as the sun and who can make me laugh through dark times.

One day a customer walked into the shop with a stack of new clothes. When Diya laid eyes on him, something sparked inside her. She couldn't understand why she was so enamoured by a man she had just met. Something about his eyes made her feel very comfortable, as if she had known him her entire life.

He dumped the clothes on the table and said he urgently needed to have his clothes altered by the next morning. He was going to Delhi for his cousin's wedding and was desperate to find someone who could help him. His mother wouldn't forgive him if he showed up in shabby clothes for the big family occasion and he would pay double if the work could be done in time. He gave Diya an endearing, little-boy smile and pleaded with her to help.

Diya was touched by his words. He was clearly one of those local college students without a woman in his life who could organize things for him. She told him to hold on a second while she ran to the back of the shop to ask her mother if they could help.

A few minutes later Diya returned with a gloomy look on her face. Unfortunately, the shop had a large order to deliver and there was no way to get to the job until the following week.

The young man's eyes became shiny, as if he was on the verge of tears. He thanked Diya for trying and, picking up his garments, headed towards the door. Diya felt terrible. There was something about the young man she found very touching. As he was leaving, she shouted for him to stop. 'I'll do it myself,' she said. 'I'm not the greatest tailor in the world but I can do a decent job. Come back tomorrow morning for your clothes.'

The man was overcome with gratitude. He took her small hands in his and brought them to his lips, giving them a delicate kiss. He introduced himself as Samar and asked her for her name. Something about him made Diya's heart race. The feeling of his lips on her skin was like nothing she had experienced before.

She told Samar that she couldn't start working on his alterations until after the shop closed and he would have to return late in the evening so she could get his measurements. Samar thanked her one more time as he left the shop.

Evening came and Diya's mother began packing up to go home. Diya, who usually helped her close down, remained in her corner. She told her mother that she had some dress patterns she wanted to make and asked if she could work late.

Shortly after the shop closed and her mother left, Diya heard a knock at the door followed by a man's voice whispering, 'It's me, Samar.'

As Diya went to the door to let Samar in, she passed by a mirror and stopped to fix her hair and adjust her blouse. It had been a long time since she had cared about how she looked and she blushed at this thought. Ignoring the butterflies in her stomach, she greeted Samar with a big smile and asked him to follow her to the fitting area so she could get his measurements.

This was the first time Diya was doing an alteration and she was nervous as she busied herself with the tape. She was aware of how dangerously close he was to her as she brushed against his body while measuring him. Her attraction to him made her feel agitated and overexcited.

Luckily, the measuring didn't take too long. When she was done, Diya managed to regain her composure and told Samar that he could leave and come back early the next morning.

Samar said he wasn't going to let her sit by herself all night, especially as she was doing him a favour. He pulled out two cold drinks from a bag and told her that she was stuck with him all night. Diya couldn't persuade him to leave; not that she tried too hard. It was turning out to be the most enjoyable evening in her life.

As she sewed, the two of them started asking each other questions about their lives. Samar was curious why a beautiful young woman like Diya was stuck working in a small sewing shop.

Too embarrassed to go into the specifics, Diya just told him that life and love had never been on her side. After many ups and downs she had learned that the world was made up of two kinds of people: those whose dreams came true and those who helped others' dreams come true. She joked that it was just like the two of them – it was her job to make sure Samar looked fabulous for the wedding he was attending.

Samar looked at her curiously, asking if that was how she really felt. He couldn't understand how someone so beautiful and kind could have such a dim view of the world. 'Life is about taking chances. You can't let the pain of the past dictate the future and, most of all, you should never be afraid to fall in love,' Samar told her.

Diya shrugged off his words. Hours went by and the two laughed and shared many stories. Finally, Diya finished the alterations and asked Samar to go into the changing area and try on his clothes.

As he came out of the fitting room, Diya stood there open-mouthed. She had never seen a man more handsome than the one standing before her. He looked like a prince from a fairy tale. Samar was delighted. He looked in the mirror and told Diya that she had done an amazing job. He went back to the dressing room and carefully took off his suit.

Exhausted, Diya rested herself on a pile of materials on the floor. Her hands were sore and her neck and back ached. She began moving her head in a circular motion, trying to relieve some of the tension. Samar sat down next to her and placed his hands on her shoulders.

'You know, I've been told I have healing hands and that in another life I must have been a masseuse,' joked Samar.

Diya giggled and told him, 'My feet are next…'

Samar had a powerful touch. As he pressed his fingers into Diya's skin she was awash with sensations she had never felt before. She could feel his warm breath on her neck as he sat just inches away from her, firmly squeezing her neck and shoulders. His touch made her feel relaxed and comfortable and caused her pain to disappear almost instantly.

Her soft skin felt like silk against Samar's fingertips. The scent of Diya's hair was like a field of flowers. It was intoxicating – he couldn't get enough.

Without warning, he kissed Diya's neck. It was so

unexpected that she jumped up and looked at him with a shocked glare.

Feeling embarrassed, Samar told her, 'I'm very sorry, I don't know what came over me. I suddenly had the urge to kiss you and I just couldn't stop myself. Please forgive me.'

'Really, it's fine, you just took me by surprise. To be honest, I was hoping you would kiss me,' Diya said. She turned bright red as soon as she uttered the words. How could she have said such a thing to a stranger? What was it about Samar that was making her break all the rules?

Samar held Diya's face with his hands and kissed her gently on the lips. Something about the act filled the empty void in Diya's heart. She responded to his kiss, her hands moving to his waist.

'I can't believe it. For so many nights I wished for the moon to send me someone to breathe life into my soul. I wished for you,' she said to him. Samar leaned over and whispered, 'I wished for you, too.'

He started kissing her neck, then moved lower. He opened her blouse and his mouth fixed on her perky breast. She tasted like sweet honey and he couldn't get enough. In his haste, he nearly tore off his own shirt.

'Be careful,' she moaned in between kisses, 'I will have to fix this too.'

Diya's body was filling with pleasure. Samar's mouth was turning her into a silken being, like the beautiful satin sarees that clients brought to the shop. She wrapped her arms tightly around his bare body and kissed him passionately. With her legs around Samar's waist she could feel his hard manhood pulsating against her skin. She began to move her lower body in a slow, circular motion, taunting him as he grew more and more anxious to be inside her.

As the passion between them grew, their bodies began to glow with sweat. Diya moved Samar so that he was on his back and sat on top of him. Samar reached up and grabbed her breasts with his strong hands, caressing and squeezing them. Diya let out a loud moan of pleasure.

They couldn't bear it any longer. Samar entered Diya. The tightness of her intimate areas sent the blood coursing through his entire body. Diya began to move her body in a gradual rhythm that drove their bodies to climax. As they came closer to ecstasy, Samar grabbed Diya's waist and began giving her steady thrusts. Diya began to moan as she inched closer and closer to climaxing. After one last thrust from Samar, they both let out a gasp and released themselves.

This had been one of the most passionate nights either of them had ever spent with anyone. They lay there all night on top of a heap of clothes, holding each other and talking about their dreams.

The next morning Diya woke up early. The shop would open in the next few hours and Samar had to leave before her mother saw him. Trying not to startle him, she whispered to her lover to wake up. Samar turned around with a yawn and wrapped his muscular arm around Diya, wishing her a sleepy good morning.

His embrace brought chills to Diya's body. She could have spent all day lying in his arms but she knew that the magical night they had shared had to come to an end. She decided to indulge herself a few moments longer before getting back to reality.

With his warm, naked body lying against hers, Samar asked Diya if she would go with him to Delhi. His train wasn't leaving until a few hours later and he offered to pay for all her expenses. He knew it was crazy but when fate brought two people together, you couldn't just walk away.

Diya was overwhelmed with different emotions.

'Last night was amazing but it was all just too perfect. That scares me. It scares me because when I felt like this earlier, men just saw it as a chance to prey on my vulnerability. I won't let another man take advantage of me…' said Diya as tears started to gather in her eyes.

Samar didn't know what to say; he couldn't understand how the passionate night they had shared had turned so quickly into something this disconnected.

'Diya, I'm not like the other men in your life. I'm sorry you had to go through such a horrible time but I'm not like those guys,' he pleaded.

Tears began to fall down Diya's face. 'Even if you're not like those other men, I'm damaged goods. You don't need a girl like me,' she said.

Samar tried to get Diya to understand that life wasn't as complicated as she was making it out to be but she wouldn't listen. She became angry and told him that he had to leave immediately.

The two got dressed quietly and made their way to the front of the store. Samar left the payment for the clothes on the counter. As he walked towards the door he turned around and told Diya, 'Not opening up yourself to love isn't going to prevent your heart from breaking…I was serious when I said that I had wished for you, too.'

As the door closed behind him, Diya fell to the floor, crying.

A few minutes later Diya's mother opened the shop and saw her daughter sobbing on the floor. She rushed to her, embraced her in a hug and asked what had happened. Diya told her everything.

'My darling daughter,' said Diya's mother. 'I know you've been hurt very badly before, but that doesn't mean everyone is going to hurt you. Sometimes you have to listen to your heart and take chances. You can't change the past chapters of your life but you can change the ones that haven't been written yet…'

'But I acted so foolishly in front of him. What am I supposed to do now?' Diya asked.

'You run. Run and don't stop until you are in his arms,' said Diya's mother, wiping the tears from her daughter's face.

Diya gave her mother a big hug and ran out of the shop. She ran so fast that she didn't look back until she had made it to the station. Just as Samar was boarding his train, he heard someone call his name. He looked around the crowded station and saw Diya.

Out of breath from running, Diya started to ramble, 'Samar, I'm so sorry. I didn't mean what I said, I was just–'

Samar interrupted her, 'Stop. Just stop.'

Diya stood there, frozen. It was too late – she had ruined whatever sparks there had been between them the previous night.

She began to plead with him but he interrupted her again. As Diya looked up at him with her big, brown eyes, he leaned down and stroked her face.

'My heart belongs to you,' he said and held out his hand to help her board the train.

The wedding was beautiful and the reception was a spectacular event. That was the last night Diya spoke to the moon...

Dear Moon,

Words cannot express how thankful I am to you. The emptiness that had consumed my heart is gone.

As long as there are stars in the sky and your light beams through the night's darkness, I will always be grateful that you granted my wish and sent me the other half of my soul.

Saying Goodbye

I want to begin by saying how deeply I miss you all. Leaving without saying goodbye was one of the hardest things I have ever done. But seeing the sadness on your faces every time I saw you just made things so difficult for me. I knew that if I stayed until the end, your final memory of me would not be of the joyful person I was so proud to be, but rather a frail, dying woman that you pitied…

If you take anything away from this story let it be this: Life is unpredictable. Don't take anyone or anything for granted and make sure to enjoy each day you have on this beautiful planet.

Maya

When I found out I had terminal cancer I cried for about a week. Once the tears dried I realized I needed to do something with the time I had left. The doctor said I had only about six months to live. I knew I didn't want to die in my apartment or in some hospital bed. I couldn't bear the thought of seeing my family and friends hovering over my sick body as I lay helpless in bed, forced to gaze into their sad faces as we said our goodbyes.

I decided to leave without telling anyone. It was hard but I knew that if people found out I was leaving they would just be upset and try to talk me out of it. They wouldn't understand that dying was something I had to do on my own terms.

I sold everything I owned, emptied out my savings accounts and took a train out of the city with only a backpack. I travelled for days, just staring out of the window, taking in the forgotten beauty of the world beyond the city. At one point the train stopped at a station in what appeared to be a tiny village.

There was a sign on the platform that said its population was only a hundred. It was a farm village – a settlement that grew vegetables to be sold in the big cities close by. There were no banks, no cinemas, not even a restaurant.

It was perfect – exactly the type of place I wanted to live out my last days. I had dreamed of building a

Saying Goodbye

beautiful garden where my body could be laid to rest. I knew this was where I would find it.

I started making my way through the village. Most people I met were curious – they weren't used to seeing strangers – but friendly. I met a woman who said her father had recently passed away and that he had left behind a farm a mile up the hill. The place was neglected and needed doing up and she offered to let me stay there for a reasonable price.

It took me a few weeks to get the property in order. The place was full of dust, spiderwebs and clutter. Once I had taken care of the mess I began working on the garden. It was tiring work but it occupied my mind and kept me busy. My fingernails were always packed with dirt and my hands sore from the constant digging. I prayed that I could find the strength to finish the garden in time.

One day as I worked I saw a man walk up to the property. He was handsome and a little rugged, probably in his twenties. He said his name was Jay and that he was looking for work. I told him I appreciated the offer but I wasn't in a position to hire anyone.

Jay said he had nowhere to go and he was desperate. Something in his pleading voice touched me, reminding me of how I had felt when I first learned my news. I didn't usually trust strangers but my instincts told me Jay was different. The best I could do, I told him, was to offer him room and board in exchange for his help in the garden. I warned him that this wasn't just a little vegetable garden but a very large project.

He thanked me eagerly and was touchingly grateful. As he walked in, I smelt alcohol on him, seeping out from his pores. I told him this was a non-drinking house and that alcohol was not permitted. Embarrassed, Jay just nodded his head and said he understood. He also told me this was just the break he was looking for and was very thankful for it.

The next day we walked down to the garden area. I showed him the plans. The garden was going to be a large square, surrounded by tall walls of flowery vines and bushes. Inside the walls would be a garden full of flowers, broken up by paths of stone running towards the centre. Here, there would be a large, empty, square patch of grass surrounded by small flowers.

Jay and I constantly bickered about how elaborate the designs for the garden were. He couldn't understand why it had to be so complicated. Certain details were just a waste of time and money in his eyes.

Saying Goodbye

I was sure that if I told him the truth he would've gone easy on me but to be honest I enjoyed the bickering. I loved getting under his skin and I could tell that he loved getting under mine. It was like we were playing a game of who could annoy the other more.

As the weeks went by, we created a great partnership, working long hours in the garden, side by side. Jay kept his promise, not touching a drop of drink, which must have been very hard. I started to feel guilty about not telling him that I was going to die. He was no longer just someone who worked for me. He had become a companion, someone I really trusted. There were days when I was on the verge of telling him but I just couldn't find the courage. I couldn't stand the idea of him looking at me with pity and sadness the way my friends and family back home had done.

The time I spent with Jay was surreal. He had come into my life at just the time I needed a companion. We spent a lot of time together just laughing and telling stories. He loved telling me obscene jokes because they always made me blush. Jay found it amusing to see me embarrassed. When I was with him, I forgot that I was dying.

One night after dinner we lay down on the porch

and stared up at the stars. We started talking about the dreams we had had as teenagers and how silly they seemed now. At one point, Jay turned his head towards me and said how great it would be for us to spend the rest of our lives together on the farm. He could see us chasing around a few children, maybe a couple of dogs.

I took a gulp of wine and tried to fight back tears. Jay could see I was upset. He asked what was wrong but I couldn't tell him. I quickly stood up and ran into the house. He followed me to my bedroom, pleading with me to tell him what he had said to make me run away. I pushed him back and yelled for him to leave.

He stood in front of me looking confused and concerned; he had never seen me that upset before. So many emotions were running through me – fear, anger, pain, sadness. I felt like I was on the verge of a breakdown.

Jay grabbed my wrists and pulled me towards him, asking me again to tell him what the matter was. I didn't have the strength to hide it from him any more – I shouted out that I was dying.

We stood there staring at one another, tears pouring down our faces. It was as if time stood still in

Saying Goodbye

that moment. I told him about my past, the doctor's verdict, why I ran away. As much as I would have loved to spend the rest of my life with Jay on the farm with children and dogs, it could never happen.

Jay came closer and, cupping my cheeks in his palms, said that no matter how many days I had left on this earth, he would cherish every one of them. He promised that he would never leave me and be right by my side when the time came.

Overcome with emotion, we grabbed each other and began kissing passionately. I had wanted to feel his lips on mine for weeks now but had never dared to think it would happen. He lay me down on the bed and asked if he could make love to me. I kissed his lips and said yes.

He took off my shirt and began caressing my body with his fingers. It had been so long since I had felt the warm touch of a man. I pulled his shirt over his head and began to explore his firm body with my hands.

His lips kissed every inch of my skin. A tingling sensation spread throughout my entire body as his soft fingers found my most pleasurable parts. As he entered me, it felt like two lost souls had finally found each other. A sense of euphoria overtook us and we lay there, gently making love with the midnight breeze for company.

We made love for hours that night but it still wasn't enough. I loved the feeling of his skin on mine – I wanted it to last forever. We fell asleep holding hands, my head resting on his chest and him stroking my hair.

The next morning, Jay woke me up with breakfast in bed. We lay there for hours, talking about life and my previous relationships. There was only one thing I was still keeping from him. I told him that it wasn't just a garden we were building. There was a reason the design was so meticulous, a reason it had to be perfect. This garden was going to be my final resting place.

I made Jay promise that when the time came for me to pass, he would take me to the garden and lay me down so I could go in peace, surrounded by nature. He agreed and said he would be right there with me the entire time.

We spent the next few months drunk in love, enjoying every moment we had left with each other.

Six months passed and the days had become more challenging. My body was deteriorating quickly. When I looked into the mirror, I could barely recognize the

Saying Goodbye

frail person staring back at me. If it wasn't for Jay, I wouldn't have survived this long.

I was now extremely weak. Jay was forced to work alone in the garden, although many of the villagers had begun to show an interest in the project and were pitching in with help. I rested on the porch most days, watching as Jay and his band completed my dream. I barely had the strength to keep writing.

Sometimes I was angry at fate. But then I thought that it was fate that had brought Jay to my door and given me the happiest moments of my life.

[Jay continues Maya's story]

Before Maya passed, she gave me this letter and asked me to finish her story. It was important for her that her family and friends back home knew why she had left so abruptly and that she hadn't died all alone.

I had never done anything for anyone, valuing people only for what they could do for me. At twenty-six, this left me a lonely drunk. Maya was the only person that made me feel like I was worthy of being loved. I never told her but the reason I had gone to the farm that day wasn't to find work. It was to kill myself.

With a pocket full of pills, I was searching for a secluded place where no one would find me. It was sheer coincidence that I wandered into Maya's farm. Maya, with her large, brown eyes, had an extraordinary effect on me from the moment I first laid eyes on her. Something about her made me change my mind and decide not to end things. It was the same instinct that made me give up drink. But it was only much later that I would be able to call it love.

As our relationship deepened, things got harder for Maya. She had a very small appetite, and when she did eat, keeping things down was difficult. Her body began to decline rapidly. Simple things like talking and getting out of bed became extremely difficult.

One morning Maya told me that it was time and she was ready. I told her to rest while I ran to the village to get a few things. I cried the entire way there and back, though I was careful to hide my tears from her.

I started getting her ready. I helped her into a beautiful white dress that someone from the village had made for her. In her hair I placed a halo I had made out of various flowers from the garden. She stood in front of the mirror and smiled. Squeezing my hand, she whispered a thank you.

I took Maya outside and we walked arm in

Saying Goodbye

arm down to the garden. The air was filled with the fragrance of fresh flowers. The sun was shining brighter than it ever had before. Butterflies danced all around us while bird calls echoed throughout the farm. It was as if Mother Nature was opening her arms to welcome Maya home.

As we made the journey we reminisced about the many happy memories we had shared. We had had so much fun working those long hours. Some days we spent more time laughing and playing than working but there hadn't been a single day that Maya didn't leave a piece of her heart and soul in that garden.

I had placed two sheer white panels at the entrance. The fabric floated prettily in the breeze and seeing them brought a smile to Maya's pain-weathered face.

As we made our way inside I revealed one last surprise for my beloved. The entire village was waiting for her. Everyone was dressed in white with flowers in their hair and around their necks.

Maya was speechless at the love she was being shown by everyone. This was the happiest I had ever seen her. Everywhere she looked there were familiar faces smiling at her and blowing kisses, each holding a single flower they had picked.

At the centre of the garden I had placed a blanket that some women from the village had sewn. I helped Maya on to it and sat down next to her. She was weak and exhausted from the walk. Using the last of her energy she looked around and lifted her frail arms, gesturing for everyone to sit down with her. It was like something out of a dream.

Maya leaned back into me and I wrapped my arms around her little body. This was how we had sat outside every night staring at the stars. Everyone just sat together, taking in all the beauty surrounding us. It should've been a sad moment but Maya's spirit made it impossible for us to feel anything but happiness.

Lying in my arms, Maya looked up at me and whispered that it was time. I began to cry. She reached up and wiped the tears from my cheek and told me not to be sad. Her body might be leaving this world but her spirit would live on in the garden forever.

As I helped her lie down I looked at her in awe. She was a vision of beauty. I gave her one last kiss so she could take with her the memory of my warm lips upon hers. It was a feeling I would never forget.

One by one the people of the village walked up to Maya, leaning down to say their goodbyes. When

Saying Goodbye

they were done each person left a single flower on top of her. Maya had no strength left to speak but in her eyes you could see just how much she appreciated their show of love.

By the end, Maya's body was completely covered in a sea of flowers. All you could see was her beautiful face. She had the most peaceful look on her face as she passed.

Maya's passing helped everyone realize how important life was, and that we should appreciate the real beauty surrounding us. As family members and neighbours stood around Maya they hugged and said how much they loved each other. Everyone's problems and worries seemed to disappear in that moment.

Maya always used to tell me that it was fate that had brought me to the farm so I could save her. It wasn't until she passed away that I realized fate had brought me to the farm, but it was so she could save me…

A Note on the Author

Actress and model, Sunny Leone has donned many hats and is known as a woman of substance. She is India's most googled person and has appeared in Bigg Boss and movies like *Jism 2* and *Jackpot*. She is also an entrepreneur and has launched her perfume line, Lust, Box Cricket League team Chennai Swaggers, and Android game Teen Patti.

juggernaut

THE APP FOR INDIAN READERS

Fresh, original books tailored for mobile and for India. Starting at ₹10.

juggernaut.in

CRAFTED FOR MOBILE READING

Thought you would never read a book on mobile? Let us prove you wrong.

juggernaut.in

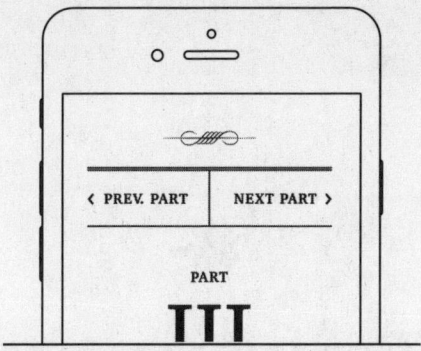

Beautiful Typography

The quality of print transferred
to your mobile. Forget ugly PDFs.

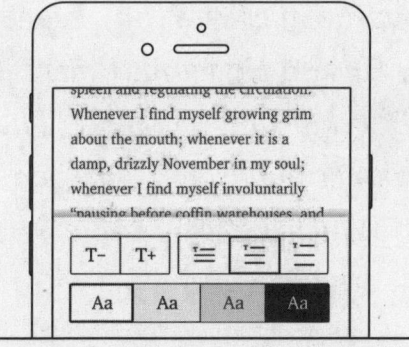

Customizable Reading

Read in the font size, spacing
and background of your liking.

juggernaut.in

AN EXTENSIVE LIBRARY

Including fresh, new, original Juggernaut books from the likes of Sunny Leone, Praveen Swami, Husain Haqqani, Umera Ahmed, Rujuta Diwekar and lots more. Plus, books from partner publishers and loads of free classics. Whichever genre you like, there's a book waiting for you.

juggernaut.in

juggernaut.in

DON'T JUST READ; INTERACT

Thought you would never read a book on mobile? Let us prove you wrong.

Ask authors questions

Get all your answers from the horse's mouth. Juggernaut authors actually reply to every question they can.

Rate and review

Let everyone know of your favourite reads or critique the finer points of a book – you will be heard in a community of like-minded readers.

Gift books to friends

For a book-lover, there's no nicer gift than a book personally picked. You can even do it anonymously if you like.

Enjoy new book formats

Discover serials released in parts over time, picture books including comics, and story-bundles at discounted rates. And coming soon, audiobooks.

juggernaut.in

4

LOWEST PRICES & ONE-TAP BUYING

Books start at ₹10 with regular discounts and free previews.

juggernaut.in

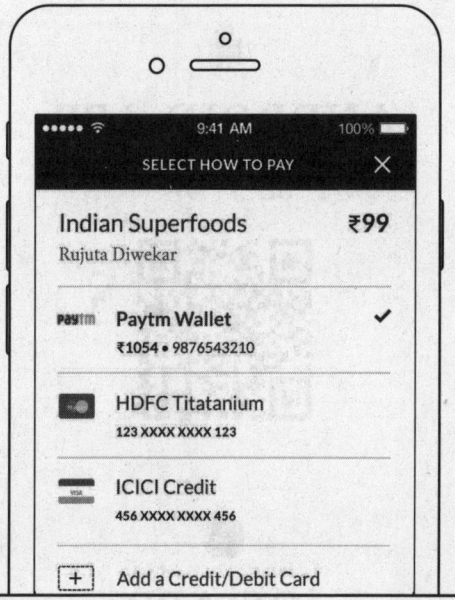

Paytm Wallet and Cards

Just connect your Paytm Wallet (or create one) once and buy any book with one tap. Or pay with your debit or credit card.

Click the QR Code with a QR scanner app or type this link into the Internet browser on your phone to download the app.

ANDROID APP
bit.ly/juggernautandroid

iOS APP
bit.ly/juggernautios

For our complete catalogue, visit www.juggernaut.in
To submit your book, send a synopsis and two sample chapters to books@juggernaut.in
For all other queries, write to contact@juggernaut.in